LITTLE MISS

VICTORIAN ROMANCE

DOLLY PRICE

PUREREAD.COM

CONTENTS

"LITTLE" BESS

There had been two boys in the family before Bess was born, and a girl born a year after her. All had been lost to sickness while Bess was still very small, so that for as long as she could remember, it had just been herself, her mother and her father.

The Lanyards lived in a small parsonage in the north of England, on a patch of land where very little grew besides the grass and the heather. Their house backed onto a great hill, or at least, it seemed great to Bess when she was growing up. She used to like scrambling up that hill, because there was a growth of dark fir trees on it, which seemed to her to provide the only proper hiding place for miles around.

Mr Lanyard, a clergyman, did not see his duties as beginning and ending behind the pulpit on Sunday, and there was seldom a time that Bess remembered in her childhood when he was not off visiting some poor family or other. She scarcely saw him, it seemed, except during their lessons together, and then he was always so grave and stern that he hardly seemed like her father at all. He taught her the Bible and read to her from Milton and Shakespeare, and her mother taught her whatever else was deemed necessary for a young girl to know—music and sewing and French.

But neither of them taught Bess how to deal with the nasty things other children said to her, or how to keep her head held high even when she was being called names. The local children had many names for her, but "little Bess" was the one she hated the most—because Bess, by the time she was ten, was taller than most girls her age, with big, clumsy hands, broad shoulders and a square jaw, and whenever she heard herself called "little," she would blush to the roots of her black hair.

For this reason, she took to avoiding town whenever she could, only venturing there for church on Sundays or when her mother sent her off to post a letter. Ashford was, to Bess, a big and dusty place, and because she had never seen any cities with which to compare it, its lanes and alleyways seemed impossibly numerous. Each corner might hold a new enemy, with some new, hurtful name to throw at her, and so Bess played most of her childhood games by herself, in the house or on the hill. Mr and Mrs

Lanyard, noticing this, thought she was just a quiet child who enjoyed her own company.

They did not know how much, in those days, Bess longed for a friend, or how, with each passing year as she grew taller and clumsier, she began to despair of ever finding one.

A THOUSAND NEW CARES

When Bess was twelve, she stopped worrying about making friends, because of a great change that took place in her life. Her father, contracting scarlet fever from a sick child on one of his charitable visits, spent months ailing in bed.

He made a brief recovery only to fall ill again after his first journey outside, and this happened several more times, so that for a whole year, Bess and her mother were kept in painful suspense. It was almost a relief when Mr Lanyard died in his sleep one night—at least, it was a relief to know that his pain was over.

But Bess and Mrs Lanyard were soon plunged into a new kind of suspense. The house was still theirs, but they could hardly afford to keep it. Mr Lanyard had left them nothing, and though the gifts of kindly neighbours sustained his widow and daughter for the first few months following his death, these soon dropped off. Bess and her mother were left to rely on their own resources. They had had to dismiss their servant, and soon they began to sell whatever furniture in the house that they could do without.

Bess, with a thousand new cares on her shoulders, did not have time to go scrambling up the hill behind their house anymore, and whenever she did venture into town, she would usually be too busy to notice the local children's taunts anymore. The children, for their part, seeing that they could not make Bess Lanyard blush or slump her shoulders no matter what they said, soon lost interest.

And so "little" Bess, at the age of thirteen, was already a young woman, and few children had ever been gladder to leave childhood behind them. Mr Lanyard had left a gap in the lives of the women in his family, it was true—but someone had to step up to fill that gap if they were going to survive.

THE CHASE

Mrs Lanyard had never been a strong woman. As long as her husband had lived, and as long as there had been a servant around who could shoulder at least some of the domestic duties, she had found herself able to manage well enough. But with Mr Lanyard dead and their servant dismissed, there was too much to do—too much to feel—too much to worry about. She sank under the weight of it all and spent months in bed.

She did not rouse herself until one January day, a year after Mr Lanyard had been lost to them. On that day, as she told her daughter later, the sun shone so bright and so clear that it seemed to beckon her out of bed, and the very wind gusting through the fir trees seemed to call out to her in her husband's voice, telling her that it was time to face the world again. Though Bess was glad to see her mother up and about again, she had so settled into her role by then, as parent and provider, that it was difficult to believe that anyone else could ever lighten the burden on her shoulders. And, at any rate, it was not to be, as her mother's months in bed had weakened her, body and mind, and she could not do half of what she had been able to do before.

Bess, all this time, had been managing, in many different little ways, to keep her and her mother alive. She had tried to find work at first, in the town and in the nearby big house, but with no references, no one would take her on, even though it was clear to them that she was a strong girl. After several wasted journeys across country, Bess had to think hard about what to do next. One Sunday, at the market in Ashford, she bought six chicken eggs with the money left over from selling some of her father's books, and carried the eggs back home carefully wrapped in her apron. Nothing had ever grown in their back garden except weeds, but Bess had a hard enough time clearing those out. It took her a whole week, and all the while she had to keep the eggs safe, tucked away in the warmest corner of the house. When the weeds had been cleared, Bess carried out her father's old desk—upturned, it would serve as a henhouse, or at least, she thought, it would be better than nothing. She didn't know anything about raising chickens, other than what she'd observed from time to time by peeping into townspeople's gardens. All she knew was that she and her mother needed some way of making money, and soon.

Four of the six eggs hatched, and soon to the sound of the wind in the firs was added a new one: a ceaseless squawking, which was so loud that Bess thought it must be heard for miles around. Venturing into town, she picked up some advice about what to feed her chickens, and made an arrangement with one of the bakers that she would collect his leftover grain once a week, in exchange for cleaning his shop floor on the apprentice's afternoon off. When the chickens began laying eggs, Bess made a little money selling them at the town market on Sundays. With that, as well as teaching music to the postmistress's daughter for an hour on Mondays, she began to make just enough to keep her and her mother afloat.

Around the same time that Mrs Lanyard was finding herself reawakening to the world around her, Bess was confronted with a new problem. One of her chickens had disappeared from the coop one night, and when she went to look the next morning and saw a trail of blood in the grass leading up to the hill, she knew that there must be a fox skulking about. She reinforced the fence around their garden, as the wood was beginning to rot, and borrowed a gun from Mr Foster's land agent at the big house. Then she posted herself in the garden after nightfall, and settled down to wait. She didn't budge from her spot even when the dark blue skies overhead opened, as they had been threatening to do all day. She just adjusted the hood of her father's old mackintosh, and kept her eyes fixed on the dark expanse of grass leading from the back garden to the hill.

After she had spent a few hours in that fashion, Bess heard the back door of the house open, and a square of light spilled out into the garden as her mother softly called, "Won't you come inside, dear? You'll catch your death."

A year before, Bess would have done as she was asked. But now she barely shifted from her position and turned her head only very slightly in the direction of her mother as she replied, "I'm doing what has to be done, Mother. Go back to bed."

After a minute or two of silence, she heard the door creaking closed, and the light retreated once more. Bess sighed, very quietly. She knew she ought to go in and apologise. But she knew she ought to stay here, too, and not risk missing her chance of getting the fox who had killed her chicken. There were so many things that she *ought* to do, and she didn't know how to set them all straight in her mind.

The night deepened, the rainfall grew harder, and Bess was beginning to despair of ever seeing her fox, when a pair of yellow, glowing eyes materialised out of the darkness just a mere few feet from her, right outside the fence. Bess was so startled that her fingers slipped as she was adjusting her grip on her gun, and the shot that was fired went right up into the air.

The glowing yellow eyes had disappeared by the time Bess scrambled to her feet, but still she gave chase up the hill, her feet sliding on the muddy ground and the hem of her mackintosh almost tripping her up at every turn.

When she came under the cover of the trees, she looked around and saw only darkness. But then, hearing a twig snap, she whirled around in the direction that she thought it must have come from, and had her gun poised to fire when she heard a very human groan.

"Help me," the voice said—it sounded like a man's.

It came from very nearby—alarmingly nearby.

Bess had gone absolutely still. "Is someone there?" she heard the man ask. As his answer was met with only silence, he groaned again and then fell silent.

Bess backed out of the trees, and nearly tumbled down the hill in her haste to get away. She didn't sleep a wink that night, and at first light was up again, armed with her gun...

THE STRANGER

The rain had stopped, and peering into her coop, she saw that her three chickens were still alive and well—the fox, evidently, had been scared enough by the gunshot not to come back. Bess's heart began to pound as she climbed the hill. She didn't know what she was more afraid of—finding the man dead, lost to the world because she had been too cowardly to help him when he had needed it, or finding the man alive and prowling around.

It didn't take much searching to find him in the copse of trees, and at first Bess thought that her first fear had been confirmed. The man was lying at the base of a tree, his head half-hidden between a twin pair of thick roots jutting out of the ground. Bess didn't take in anything about his appearance beyond that he was filthy and mud-soaked; her first priority was seeing if he was still alive, and once she had crouched by his side and heard his faint, laboured breathing, her own breath whooshed out of her lungs.

She got an arm around his shoulders and heaved him into a sitting position. His head lolled, wings of lank blond hair brushing his jawbone, and Bess could see now, under the layer of dirt, that he was younger than she had thought. "Sir?" she said, cautiously. He groaned in response but did not lift his chin or open his eyes. She tried again. "Sir?"

"I've been here all night," he murmured. One of his limp hands began patting the soil beside him. "Only bit of shelter… I could find… for miles around."

"Yes, it is," Bess agreed. "I'm sorry I didn't come to help you sooner. I heard you crying out last night, but I was scared."

The young man seemed to find this funny. "Scared of me?" he repeated and gave a dry laugh that sounded like it had been wrenched from somewhere deep in his body. "Well, I won't hurt you. I don't hurt anyone but myself."

Bess didn't really understand this, nor did she have time to puzzle out its meaning. "There's a house on the other side of this hill. My house. I can get you down there, but you'll have to help me. I don't think I can lift you all by myself."

The young man's blond eyelashes fluttered, and when he opened his eyes at last, they were of such a light blue that they stood out startlingly in his dirty face. Those eyes fixed on Bess, and he said consideringly, "You look strong."

"I'm not *that* strong," Bess said firmly. "Please, sir, you'll have to try your best to walk. It's only a short way down."

The man's eyelashes were already fluttering closed again. "Sir," she said, and he blinked a few times.

"Yes, yes, all right." Together they heaved him up onto his feet. His breath came out in short, painful gasps as they began to move, but Bess, looking sidelong at him, couldn't tell where he might be injured. She couldn't see anywhere that was bleeding, and he was not walking with a limp, just with painful hesitance in putting one foot in front of the other.

"Talk to me," said the young man, as they made their slow progress along. "It'll help me stay awake."

"What shall I talk about?" said Bess, gritting her teeth as he made a movement that sank more of his weight on her.

"Tell me a story. Your story."

Bess looked down at the ground. "Very well."

MOTHER'S INSTINCT

I t had taken only a few minutes for Bess to tell the young man the story of herself, her mother and father, and those siblings of hers who had not followed her to adulthood. But it took a whole week before the young man, who was called Tom Steele, would tell Bess *his* story. Even once it had been told, Mrs Lanyard was quite sure that some important details had been left out.

"He says that he was shooting with his friends," she said, approaching Bess one day at the door of the guest room where they had decided to put the young man. "And that he got separated from his party and fell off his horse. But what would they be shooting at this time of year? Pheasant, grouse? No birds like that to be found in these parts."

Bess glanced anxiously towards the door of the guest room, which stood ajar, and was reassured by the sound of soft, steady breathing, which informed her that her charge was still asleep. "There are pheasant in the woods on the Fosters' estate," she told her mother. Bess knew this because she had spoken to one or two men in town who poached in those woods, and had, once or twice during her desperate search for food, been tempted to join them. She had only been prevented from doing so because her fear of getting caught had outweighed her fear of going hungry. "Maybe Mr Steele was shooting around there."

Mrs Lanyard shook her head at once. "I met the Fosters' housekeeper in town yesterday and asked her about him. She says she never heard of a Mr Steele. He's no friend of the Fosters, that's for sure."

Bess was at a loss for words for a moment. With another glance towards the door to the guest room, she said with resignation, "You shouldn't be going in town yet, Mother. You're not strong enough."

Mrs Lanyard put a hand to her daughter's arm, forcing her attention back on her. Bess looked at her in surprise. "I know I haven't been what I ought to be, to you, since…"

"We don't have to discuss it," said Bess, quickly.

"But you must listen to me now," her mother went on. "I've seen many men like him before. Very well, I'll believe that he fell from his horse: he has the bruises to prove it.

But whether he was shooting or drinking—I think it much more likely to be the latter."

"You don't know that," Bess argued.

"But I do know that he's been asking you to sneak him a glass of sherry from my cabinet every night." Mrs Lanyard paused as she watched the colour flood her daughter's face. "Did you think I wouldn't notice?"

"I only took a little bit to him, a few times," Bess said feebly. "He said he needed it… for the pain…"

"Yes, I'm sure it *is* painful," said her mother, "to break the habits of self-indulgence and debauchery. I told you, Bess, I've seen many young men like him before. What do you think happens to a person, when they have always been given everything they have ever wanted, had every whim satisfied and every desire fulfilled? Their soul becomes more and more greedy; they can never learn to be content with what they have."

FRIENDS

B ess had heard many such sermons from her
father before. She knew the truth of them, but
she found it hard to reconcile that truth with the
young man who was staying in their house.

First of all, there was his appearance: the blond locks of
hair and smooth face, the soft white hands and perfect
pink fingernails, all of which, once the dirt of the road had
been cleaned away, combined to make him look almost
angelic. This was especially the case when he was
sleeping, and since he was very ill for the first few days
after Bess found him on the hill, that was most of the time.

But of course, she had also been taught to look beyond
appearances, not just by her father's sermons, but by her
own hard experiences. No matter how good and kind she
had always tried to be, that had not stopped the children
in town from calling her cruel names, because of things

that she could not control—because she was tall and clumsy. Because of that, Bess was in no danger of falling into such a mistake herself, of judging people solely by how they looked.

But Tom Steele was not just handsome. He was many other things, too, which Bess soon discovered during the week that followed her finding him on the hill.

Even before he had told her his story—the story that her mother believed to be missing many important details, the story of his being the heir to an estate in Somerset, and having come to the north to visit one of his friends, where he ended up getting separated from a shooting party and getting stranded in the bad weather—Bess had observed some things about him. She saw, by the rings on his finger and the pocket-watch that she found in his mud-soaked waistcoat, that he must indeed come from a rich family. So, it naturally followed that he must be used to much more comfortable surroundings than their guest room, which had by now been stripped of most of its furniture apart from the bed. But Tom Steele never complained, never asked probing questions about her and her mother's reduced circumstances.

What made this even more remarkable was that he asked a great deal of other questions, especially as he began to recover some of his strength and spend less and less time asleep.

He asked about what books Bess was reading, about what music she was teaching the postmistress's daughter in town, and whether it was the same as the kind of music that she really liked to play. He asked about her favourite passages from the Bible and compared them with his own. He asked what kind of a man her father had been and listened carefully as she described how charitable he had been, how much he had taught her. "But didn't he ever play any games with you?" was one of the first questions Tom asked which really startled Bess, because it forced her to stop and consider. When a minute's thoughtful silence had passed, she confessed that all of her childhood games had been solitary ones, and Tom gave a sad kind of smile and nodded. And the strangest thing of all was that he seemed to have already understood everything without her having to tell him: about the cruel children in town, about her longing for a friend, about any of it.

ONE MORE DROP

Bess knew that, since he came from the south, Tom must not be used to the north wind that whistled through their bare house, or the squalls of rain that would come sweeping across the country, lashing against the windows that had shown a blue sky five minutes before. But he never complained about that either and showed his discomfort only by the occasional shiver. Bess filled hot water bottles for him, brought old shawls and blankets to layer over his coverlet, but he had never asked her to do any of those things: the only favour he had begged, indeed, was that of the glass of sherry every night, and she had been glad to oblige until her conversation with her mother. That night, when he made his usual request, she reluctantly gave a different answer.

"We've run out, I'm afraid, Mr Steele," she said, and busied herself adjusting the loose latch on the window, so that she would not have to see his reaction. She felt his eyes on her all the same, and at length when she turned to go, he said,

"This is because of what your mother said, isn't it?"

Bess turned again and stared at him. "You mean—you heard? I was sure you were asleep!"

"I was pretending, I'm afraid," he said, with an apologetic quirk of his lips. "You see, I never could resist eavesdropping on any conversation that concerned me. I hope you can forgive me."

"If you can forgive *me*," said Bess, not quite meeting his gaze as she moved towards the end of the bed and straightened an imaginary wrinkle on the coverlet.

"There's nothing *to* forgive. Your mother was quite right: I didn't tell you my whole story."

Bess went still, and chanced a glance towards him as she asked, "Why not?"

Tom raised his eyes to the ceiling, evidently considering his answer. "Well, it's not that I'm ashamed. Really I *should* be, but I've never learned yet how to regret doing what gives me pleasure. I like to drink, and when my friends are drinking, too, it's even better. That's what we were all doing, at my friend Harry's house some ways north of here, when I took it into my head to go for a ride in the middle of the night. I must have fallen asleep in the saddle, and my horse threw me somewhere—I don't know where. I was wandering for a long time before you found me."

Bess was silent. "Are you shocked?" Tom asked.

"Not shocked," she said, after a moment's consideration. "More... sorry."

"Sorry for me? But you don't have to be. I assure you, I was having a splendid time right up until I fell off that horse. And I intend to go on having more splendid times, as soon as I've got a bit of strength back."

"Will you go back?" Bess had moved to sit in the chair by his bedside, leaning slightly forward with her hands folded in her lap. "To your friend's house?"

"No." Tom gave a rueful laugh. "I think I'm in too much trouble to do that. Harry will have told my family by now that I'm missing, you see. And it's not the first time it has happened—so really I'm hiding here until the worst has blown over. By then, I hope they'll be so glad to see me again that they won't be too angry. Though you never know with the Earl."

Bess had learned by now that this was how Tom always referred to his father, and there seemed to her to be something impertinent in the way he said it. But there was something else in his speech that had concerned her even more. "You shouldn't play with their feelings like that. I'm sure they *are* very worried about you—so you ought at least to write and tell them that you are all right."

"And send them running here? Your mother wouldn't thank me for that. And they wouldn't thank you, either of you, even though you *have* taken such good care of me." Tom shifted around on his pillows. "No, I'd like to have a little bit longer before I have to face them." He glanced at her. "That is, if it's not an imposition."

"You're welcome to stay here as long as you like, Mr Steele," said Bess at once.

"It's all very well for you to say that, but what about your mother?"

"It's my decision to make," said Bess. "Not hers."

Tom raised his eyebrows and blew out his breath. "Well. I say, couldn't you go and face my father in my place? It'd make my job a great deal easier. I'm sure he wouldn't dare to question you, if you told him I've decided to live here, in…"

"Ashford," Bess supplied, unable to hide her smile.

"… in Ashford, with my very good friends the Lanyards, for the rest of my days. How about that?"

"That would be nice," Bess said quietly, the trace of a smile still lingering on her lips.

"Yes, it would, wouldn't it?" Tom sighed, and then turned towards her. "But since it isn't possible, what about getting me that glass of sherry instead?"

Bess met his look of appeal, nodded, and, for a moment, let herself bask in the grateful glow of his countenance. Then she got up and moved for the door. "I can only get you a little bit, or my mother will notice."

"A little bit is all I ask," Tom called after her, and she shook her head in feigned exasperation before closing the door.

THE PROMISE

That conversation had done more than confirm Bess's mother's suspicions. It had reminded Bess of the reality that, up until now, she had been reluctant to acknowledge: that Tom Steele would not be here forever, that he belonged somewhere else and would very soon be forced to return to his responsibilities there.

The next morning, before anyone else in the house was awake, she got up and climbed the hill outside. She sat under the shelter of the fir trees, with her long legs awkwardly crossed in front of her—sat and thought, until she could feel the cold dew seeping into the underside of her skirt. Only then did she get up and go back down to the house.

She knew, by then, what she wanted to tell Tom, but it took her two more days to work up the courage to say it.

Then, when she finally managed to open the conversation, it didn't go quite the way she had expected.

"I wanted to ask…" she began, and let the words hang there, miserably, until Tom prompted,

"Ask me anything, and I'll grant it. I shouldn't say that, of course, without knowing what is being asked first. But there you are. And I would advise you to take advantage of my generosity, while it lasts." He laughed. He was laughing a great deal today, for, thanks to the thaw that had come in the weather over the past few days, they had taken an experimental walk around the moors, and Bess could tell that the fresh air was doing Tom a world of good.

"When you go back," Bess went on, with difficulty, "I'll miss you." She grimaced as soon as the words were out and waited for him to recoil or make fun of her.

"I'll miss you, too," said Tom, in a tone that suggested her sentiment to be a perfectly natural one. "Heaven knows you're more interesting to talk to than most young ladies my age. You know a great deal more than them, too. Are you quite sure you're only fourteen?"

"Thirteen," Bess corrected him, though it gave her pain to do so. "I'll be fourteen in March."

"Thirteen! Well, you've got it all ahead of you. And what do you plan to do with yourself when you're older?"

Bess wasn't quite sure how, but the conversation seemed, very quickly, to have run away from its intended direction. "What… what do you mean?"

"Well, you don't intend to hide yourself away here for the rest of your life, do you?" Tom swept a glance over the bare land surrounding them. "You should ask your mother to bring you to London, once you're old enough."

"I don't think that would be possible."

"Oh, it's not so very expensive, I promise you. Especially if you only spend a season there. You can get cheap lodgings in Holborn or somewhere. There are subscriptions to pay for the balls, and the opera, but you don't need to concern yourself with that. The real quality go to the private parties, and those are free: all you need is a nice gown or two and an introduction. I can help with the introduction part of things. All you'll have to do is write to me whenever you're coming."

"You're very kind," said Bess, who was blushing now, "but I really don't think it will be in my power, or Mother's. You see, as soon as I'm old enough, I'm going to go out as a governess."

"A governess!" Tom repeated, and looked at her, aghast. "Why are you—why on earth would you—"

"My mother doesn't like it either," Bess spoke with forced calm, as the look on his face made her feel ashamed and uncertain. "But I've decided it's the only thing to do. It's the only way a young lady like me can make a respectable living."

"Not the only way," Tom countered. "You could be a companion or—or write novels, for heaven's sake. *Anything* but be a governess. Why, if you marry well, you won't have to make a living at all."

"None of those things are certainties," Bess pointed out. "To be a companion, you need connections. To write novels, too, and you have no guarantee that anyone will even read them. And as for marrying well…" She was unable to voice the end of that thought out loud. Thankfully, Tom didn't seem to notice.

"So you'll hire yourself out instead? You'll place yourself at the mercy of some rich, vulgar family, charged with the education of their unruly children, who—well, you'll forgive me for saying this, but if they're anything like me and my brothers were, I doubt you'll be able to teach them anything at all!" Tom shook his head, looking almost angry. "It's not fair."

"It's the way things are," Bess said quietly.

"But it doesn't have to be. I could help you, you know." He halted in his tracks and turned towards her, his face brightening. "Yes, I could help you! I could give you and your mother a reward, for finding me and saving me. It's what I was intending to do, in any case. How much will you need, to keep you from having to hire yourself out?"

"I—" Bess had already begun to shake her head.

"Of course, you'll refuse, and say you don't expect any reward, and all of that," Tom rushed on. "And so will your mother. But you haven't encountered my stubbornness. Once I get an idea in my head, you see, I never let go of it. So, you're to write to me as soon as I get back to Branledge, and we'll arrange it all."

"My mother won't accept any sum from you, and I'm sure I can't either…"

"Yes, yes; like I said, you're wasting your words."

"… but I *would* like to keep in touch," Bess finished. She sensed Tom glance at her, in evident surprise at the change in her tone. "I like—talking to you. There aren't many people here, who I can…"

"Of course not, when you hide yourself away up here." Tom tapped her shoulder, very lightly. "We'll promise to stay friends, then?"

Bess met his gaze and nodded. For a moment she wished she could be just like him, letting her emotions play right on the surface just as he did, speaking an emotion as soon as she felt it. If she had been more like Tom Steele, then she would have been able to clap her hands and jump up and down on the spot just then, just as she wanted to. As it was, she had to content herself with a small smile.

"I've been told I'm not the best correspondent," Tom went on as they started walking again, "But for your sake, Bess, I will try to reform myself."

THE BAXTER'S OF THIS WORLD

After Tom Steele had left the Lanyards' house, they did not hear from him again.

He did not write to them once, not even to send a note to let them know that he had arrived home safely, once that certain period of time had elapsed after which Bess supposed that he must have. She had not taken his words about the reward seriously, but she *had* hoped that he would write.

"Out of sight, out of mind," was her mother's matter-of-fact conclusion, but Bess couldn't believe that—at least, not at first. It took a long time before she could walk into the post office in town with any sense of calm, and even longer before she stopped feeling her heart sink upon hearing that same, dreaded response from the post-mistress: "No letters."

Her lessons with the post-mistress's daughter had stopped by then, as Sally, now ten, was declared a lost cause: she had no patience for music and no hope of being made to like it, despite Bess's best efforts. This loss of income gave Bess one or two sleepless nights, but Mrs Lanyard, while not sufficiently strong enough to go out to work herself, had taken a few measures in that direction, including taking on a couple of gentlemen's daughters as pupils. These were local girls whose fathers could not afford to send them to a young ladies' school, and who had been sent to Mrs Lanyard instead on the strength of her late husband's reputation as a learned man.

Thankfully, not all of his books had been sold by Bess, and Mrs Lanyard was quite well-read enough to supply the gap left by those that had. The girls got their bed and board for free, and paid Mrs Lanyard only for their lessons, but this was still a steadier income than she or her daughter had received for years.

Bess, who still had a few years of learning ahead of her before she could go out to teach, often sat in on these lessons with the other two girls. But she did not find a friend in either Miss Collins or Miss Baxter, both of whom had been members of the group of town children that had once tormented Bess. They still tittered behind their hands whenever she tripped over a chair leg or dropped a book, and when Mrs Lanyard had left the room, they would call Bess some of those names she had almost forgotten.

Bess did not tell her mother, as she knew that there was nothing to be done; they needed the girls' money, and if she had to put up with some little trials in order to get it, she would grit her teeth and do exactly that. She got through the worst of the indignities by fixing her mind on that time which was coming up soon: the time when she would be independent and free from all the Collinses and Baxters of the world.

SILENCE AND SUFFERING

T hose two short weeks when Tom Steele had been staying with them remained fresh in Bess's mind and seemed likely to do so no matter how much time passed. It could not be otherwise. Whatever about the silence that had followed his departure, when Tom had been here, Bess had felt what it was to have a friend. Nothing could spoil that memory; nor, it seemed, could anything uproot the seed of hope that he had planted within her.

She was always hoping, whenever she looked into the face of a boy or young man, to find a certain pair of blue eyes staring back at her, but the eyes that stared at her instead, blue, or green or brown, held none of his warmth or humour.

When Bess was seventeen, she put out an advertisement in the county paper, offering her services at the highest rate that she could, which, given the fact that she had no references, was only twenty pounds a year.

Her mother offered to help, suggesting that it would be easier to find a situation closer to home, where the name of "Lanyard" might afford Bess some consideration, but Bess was firm on this point: she would not take any situation in Ashford. She had only just gotten away from Miss Collins and Miss Baxter—she was not about to land herself teaching the younger brothers or sisters of any of her childhood tormentors. It took months and months of her mother and herself writing letters, however, and several more newspaper advertisements, before something at last appeared for Bess. She was to teach the two young children of a squire named Wallace, in a market town twenty miles away.

Bess went forth to Hartleton with rather less fear or anxiety than any other young woman would have felt in her position. It was true that she had never been so far from home, but with such a childhood as she had had, filled with loneliness and punctuated by grief and hardship, she felt that there was not much in the world left for her to fear.

She had no idea that more punishment awaited her, but by the end of her first week working in Mr Wallace's house, Tom's long-ago words had come back to her with a vengeance. *You'll place yourself at the mercy of some rich, vulgar family, charged with the education of their unruly children? I doubt you'll be able to teach them anything at all.*

Tom had not meant the words unkindly, back then, of that Bess was sure, but living in the Wallaces' home for the first time, she felt a bit of resentment creep into her memory of her friend, because he had been right about all of it.

The children, two young girls of four and six, were unteachable. They screamed when Bess tried to teach them to sing and scratched at her when she tried to get them to write sums on their slates. They had no father to discipline them, at least, none that Bess had ever seen, for in all the time that she was working there, she never saw Mr Wallace.

Mrs Wallace's movements were also mysterious to her, but at the very least, she could be counted on to make an appearance at least once a day. She took a dislike to Bess from the moment she arrived, after the latter accidentally trod on the hem of her gown: indeed, all such accidents of Bess's clumsiness seemed only to confirm her incompetence to Mrs Wallace. Mrs Wallace, of course, didn't talk to her own children if she could help it, and her placid expression never changed no matter how much noise they were making.

The only person in the household, it seemed, who could make the little Wallace girls listen, was the young footman. He was like an older brother to them, calming them in their tantrums or tousling their hair when they were being naughty.

He was also the only person who came to bid Bess goodbye when, at the end of three months, she was told that her services were no longer required. Standing in the drive in front of the house, he helped her up into the farmer's cart that was to take her home and handed her her valise. "You tried, miss," he told her regretfully, and his face blurred before Bess in her mist of tears. "You tried your best. Everyone knows it."

TEARS

B ack home, Bess handed over to her mother the envelope containing her measly earnings: six pounds four shillings. Mrs Lanyard, to her credit, did not say "I told you so." But when she offered, gently, to make some inquiries closer to home this time around, Bess felt the sting all the same. She nodded, excused herself, and went outside to climb her hill. Only when she was under cover of the trees did she let her tears flow freely.

THE FOSTERS

The Fosters, who owned the big house and much of the land around Ashford, had only one daughter, who was a couple of years younger than Bess. It had been generally accepted that this daughter would be sent to school in London, and as such, Mrs Lanyard had never considered the Fosters when making her inquiries. But in the time that Bess had been away teaching in Hartleton, Mrs Foster had passed away after a long illness, and Mr Foster, wanting to keep his daughter close to his side, had decided that it was now out of the question to send her to school.

Hearing that Mrs Lanyard's daughter was a governess in search of a new situation, he called on them at the parsonage one day, and so, a mere week after Bess had been dismissed by the Wallaces, she had found a new position at Ashford Hall.

Bess's new pupil, while certainly a lot less trouble than the Wallace girls had been, did not seem to see herself as a pupil at all, or Bess as a governess. From the first day, when Laura Foster showed up late for her lesson and collapsed into the chair opposite Bess in a flounce of skirts, that much became clear.

"I know this already," Laura grumbled when Bess started talking about the subjunctive tense in French. "I've read them already," was the response when Bess produced a book of Wordsworth's poems, and sure enough, when questioned, Laura was able to recite the greater part of *Lines Composed a Few Miles above Tintern Abbey.* She had no patience for geography, either, insisting that anyone could point to New Zealand on a map. While Bess was running through the other subjects, trying to get a sense of how much Laura knew already, she sensed the other girl watching her.

"Aren't you supposed to be a clergyman's daughter?" Laura demanded, as soon as Bess stopped to draw breath.

"My father was a clergyman, yes, Miss Foster."

"But you haven't mentioned God or the Bible once."

"If you like I could talk about the Bible with you," Bess said, unable to hide her own eagerness. "We could start with the Psalms…"

"No, goodness, no, I get enough of that at church on Sunday." Laura settled back in her chair and drew up her legs in front of her chest, evidently so intent on making herself comfortable that she didn't care whether her petticoats showed. "No, I'm only trying to puzzle out in my head why Father took you on. I wonder if he wants me to be more holy. Or maybe he just thought I could use some company—this house *has* been pretty gloomy lately."

"Your father took me on," said Bess, as calmly as she could, "to be your governess, Miss Foster, and that is the role I intend to perform."

"You be *my* governess! But you can't be much more than seventeen, eighteen! What on earth can *you* teach *me*?"

"Well, since I am sure that there must be some books that you haven't read already, and some subjects in which you can still be instructed…"

"Miss Lanyard, I am telling you this because I think it will save us both a great deal of time." Still lolling back in her chair, Laura fixed her governess with a look of sympathy. "You don't have to teach me anything. No one expects it. My mother—if she was still alive—wouldn't expect it: she only wanted me to go to school to pick up a bit of needlework. And my father certainly doesn't expect it. As for me, well, I think, since we're around the same age, you and I would be better off being friends."

Bess was gazing at the other girl in disbelief, wondering how she could talk so calmly about her mother's recent death. Laura, noticing her gaze, went on, "You don't have to take all of this so seriously. All you have to do is show up whenever I call you, talk to me and amuse me."

"I am not being paid to amuse you," Bess said, firmly. "I am being paid to instruct you."

"Talk to my father, then." Laura rose from her chair with a sigh and stretched languidly. "Tell him I'm an unwilling pupil, if you like. See if he cares."

"Where are you going, Miss Foster?" Bess demanded, getting to her feet. Laura had already reached the door of the schoolroom, and threw back over her shoulder,

"I'm going for a walk, Miss Lanyard. As the fresh air will be very good for me, I'm sure you can't object."

TAKING CHARGE

Since Ashford Hall was almost five miles distant from the parsonage, making it too far for Bess to walk there and back every day, she had been given a room near the servants' quarters, and only saw her mother once a week for Sunday dinner. During her first such dinner, she told Mrs Lanyard all about her new, difficult pupil, and was surprised by the lack of sympathy she got from her mother.

"All she wants is discipline," said Mrs Lanyard, with a shrug. "You must show her that you're in charge. Make her sit and listen while you are teaching. Forbid her to go for walks during your lessons."

"But it's not as easy as that…"

"How do you think *I* manage it? Did you ever see Miss Collins or Miss Baxter walking out during one of my lessons?"

"No, but that's different," Bess protested. "You are older, so they found it natural to listen to you. The trouble with Miss Foster is that she and I are almost the same age…"

"That ought to make it easier. Think of the trouble you had with those very young girls at the Wallaces. A pupil closer to your age ought to be easier to manage."

This stumped Bess. She dropped the subject but lingered over her meal for as long as she could and stayed to help her mother wash the plates in the scullery. She was on the point of offering to feed the chickens when her mother, glancing at the kitchen clock, said, "Shouldn't you be getting back to Ashford? It will be dark in an hour."

THE MASTER OF THE HOUSE

Night had fully fallen by the time Bess came in sight of the woods that surrounded the Fosters' grand house from view. She had spun out the time for as long as she could at home, and then dawdled so much on the five-mile walk back, because there was nothing she was dreading more than her return to Ashford Hall. It was not just Miss Foster's intractability; it was the place itself.

Bess had not realised, until she had escaped to the parsonage today, what a cloud she had been living under for the past week. She had not realised how unnaturally silent the place was, nor tasted the sourness on the air, nor noticed the weight of some great emotion pressing down on her shoulders. But all those sensations attacked her now as she stepped under the threshold of the great house. Had their own house been like this, after her father had died? Bess struggled to think, but couldn't remember: that time, for her, came up as a blur of activity and bustle.

It made her tired, and she was crossing the hall with the intention of going straight to her room, when she saw, through the open door to the dining room, Mr Foster sitting in an armchair close to the fire, with his pointer sleeping at his feet and a skein of cigar smoke curling above his head.

Shy of Mr Foster as Bess was—she had only spoken a handful of words to him since she had been taken on; he hadn't even interviewed her on her arrival—she could not pass up an opportunity such as this. During the week, at least for the brief times that she had glimpsed him, he always seemed too busy with something or other, striding through the grounds with his land agent or shut up in his library with his solicitor. But now he was alone, and apparently unoccupied. Bess stepped up to the open door, and paused, and then took the plunge.

"Mr Foster, sir?"

He turned to look at her as she entered the circle of firelight, and she saw that, while he held a cigar in one hand, he was holding a glass of spirits in the other. His fair skin was blotchy, his grey eyes bloodshot, and as those eyes narrowed on her, Bess had the sudden sense that she had strayed into a domain where she did not belong.

"Mr Foster," she said again, folding her hands over her front. "I am sorry to disturb you, but I wanted to talk to you about your daughter."

Mr Foster took a puff of his cigar and then looked back at her as he tapped the ash out onto the hearth.

"I'm afraid—" Bess went on, "that I am finding it difficult to discipline her. She doesn't seem willing to learn at all. I was wondering, sir, if you might be willing to have a word with her."

The expression in Mr Foster's eyes was utterly blank. Thinking that she mustn't have made herself clear enough, Bess rushed on, "I know, of course, sir, that it is my task to discipline her, and I have been doing my best— and I will carry on doing my best. That goes without saying. I only think that, as her father, you might have some influence with her that I can't—that might help…"

"Miss Lanyard," said Mr Foster, in a voice slightly hoarse, as though from lack of use. He took a sip from his glass and grimaced, whether from the bitter taste or strength of the liquor, Bess was not sure. "Go to bed."

"V-very good, sir." Bess, in her confusion, gave a half-curtsy, and turned on her heel. She felt Mr Foster's eyes follow her all the way out of the room.

A SMALL VICTORY

Since there was evidently no hope of Mr Foster helping her, Bess was forced upon other methods, during the second week of her employment, to try to impart any kind of learning to Laura. At first, she tried acting on her mother's instructions, and exerting her authority—this mainly consisted in raising her voice whenever Laura tried to interrupt, tapping the desk with her ruler whenever Laura found herself distracted by some more interesting object outside the window, or, in cases of extremity, forbidding Laura from leaving the house until she had finished such and such an exercise.

This last measure Bess hoped to have some effect, since she had discovered by now that one of Laura Foster's chief pleasures in life was to be looked at, and whether walking along the country lanes or into town, she was sure of at least some admirers. Within the confines of

Ashford Hall, on the other hand, there were only the servants, and Laura did not count them as admirers.

The trouble was that Laura, even after being expressly forbidden from doing something, would just go and do it anyway.

Bess had no idea how to exert her authority when it was so blatantly ignored like that. Beyond locking the schoolroom door, or dragging Laura kicking and screaming away from the front door of the house, neither of which were things that Bess would dare to do, there seemed to be nothing else that would ensure her pupil's obedience of her. Some of the time it was as if Bess did not exist—but, in fact, it was worse than that; because far worse than not existing was existing and being ignored.

Determined to finish their lessons but helpless against Laura's whims, Bess would often be forced to take up her books and follow Laura wherever, continuing to read aloud or test her on some conjugation or definition, while Laura plucked idly at her harp or went wandering through the grounds. It was on one chilly afternoon, as they were walking with the autumn leaves spinning down around them, that Bess suddenly felt herself boiling over with resentment.

Maybe it was the fact that she didn't have good gloves like Miss Foster did, and could feel the skin of her hands roughening in the raw air; maybe it was the insolent smile playing around Laura's lips as Bess talked; maybe it was the way that she kept interrupting Bess to greet some passing tenant, or to point out some improvement that her father had made to an orchard wall here, or a cottage roof there.

But if Bess was honest with herself, what she began feeling, in that moment, went much deeper than that. Bess had never forgotten the things that had been told to her in childhood: that she was big, and awkward, and clumsy, and not what an elegant young lady should be at all. Next to Laura Foster, she felt all of those things, and worse. Laura, only fifteen, was already a beauty, and she knew it. With her soft, fair hair, her dimples, her narrow waist and small, delicate wrists, she drew the eye immediately, whether in envy or admiration.

For Bess, it was mostly the former. She had noticed it in the sinking of her heart on the first day that she had been introduced to her pupil, and she noticed it now, in the way that her face suddenly felt very hot, and in the way that all of her body seemed to have tightened, and in the way that she could not so much as look in Laura's direction without being seized by the urge to pull one of her fair ringlets.

"Oh, there's a lovely little path I never saw before," Laura was saying, pointing through the trees. "Let's go and see where it leads." But she had scarcely taken one step in that direction when Bess seized hold of her arm.

Laura turned to stare at Bess. "Why, Miss Lanyard! How dare you? Let go of me!"

"You are not going down that path," Bess told her, in a voice as sharp as a whip, "because you will only get your dress muddy, just as you did yesterday and the day before, and then the maids will have to clean it, just as they did yesterday and the day before, and they will come complaining to *me* because I can't manage you properly, and—tell me, Miss Foster, do you *ever* think of anybody but yourself?"

Laura Foster's lovely grey eyes, now wide with disbelief, remained fixed on Bess for a moment longer. "Well," she said after a moment, and, as Bess released her arm, made a show of straightening her sleeve. "Well, I'm sure I have no wish to cause any trouble." She turned away from the proposed path, and back in the direction of the house. Bess followed a little way behind, divided between shame and wonder at what she realised to be her first victory over her pupil.

But Bess could not really be proud of a victory won in such a manner. She had not exerted her own authority in a calm and cool way, as she knew her mother would have done; instead she had lashed out in anger at a girl who was younger than her, a girl who was under her charge, a girl who could not help that she was beautiful—even if Bess did feel, in her worst moments, as though Laura existed just to torment her.

MR NEWMAN

When she accompanied Miss Foster to church the following Sunday (Mr Foster never joined them, and had never done so, Bess was informed, even prior to Mrs Foster's death), Bess resolved to use the time to reflect on her own poor conduct.

She had relieved her own conscience a little by apologising to Laura after her outburst a few days ago, and her apology had been graciously accepted, but the uncomfortable feelings which had provoked that outburst were still there, swirling and boiling around inside Bess. As she took her place in the pew beside Laura, she folded her hands in her lap and fixed her gaze on the empty pulpit. For a minute or two, the church around her dimmed, and the noise faded to a low buzz of conversation. But then Laura nudged her, and Bess was jolted back to reality. "It's him," her charge hissed in her ear. "Mr Newman."

Laura was not the only excited one; the low buzz rose to a rumble as the sound of footsteps came up the aisle. Bess felt it would compromise her dignity to crane her neck around to get a good look at the young minister, as half of the other churchgoers were doing, including Laura. But she was curious nonetheless, as her pupil had already told her a great deal about Mr Newman.

He was the curate, who had started at the church at Ashford while Bess had been away teaching the Wallaces, and who had been absent last Sunday, meaning that this was Bess's first opportunity of seeing him. The moment was less significant to her than it evidently was to Laura, who was anxious to get Bess's opinion on Mr Newman, and kept nudging her throughout the service, until Bess was nearly put out of patience. Her resolve to reflect on her own conduct over the past week was soon broken down, as it was all she could do to focus on the minister's words with Laura squirming and fidgeting in the seat beside her.

"Well?" Laura demanded, after the last hymn had been sung and they were filing out of church. "What do you think? Is he not handsome?"

Bess looked around, and waited until they were out of earshot of the family behind them in the aisle before she replied, "Yes—in a certain way."

"'In a certain way'? He's so tall and imposing! And that dark brow of his, that makes him look so serious when he speaks, and his eyes, so alive with expression—and his voice, Miss Lanyard, did you ever hear anything like it?"

"No," Bess admitted, squinting as they emerged into the sunlight. "He certainly speaks very well."

"'Very well'? So this is your praise of him? I wonder if you can feel at all, Miss Lanyard! Why, every time he opened his mouth, I felt this thrill all over me. And when he looked at me at the end of his sermon, I thought I might die right there on the spot."

"You mustn't say things like that, Miss Foster."

"But it's true! Why shouldn't I be honest? You did see him looking at me those other times, too, didn't you?"

"I did," said Bess, reluctantly, for she had noticed that the minister's eyes—eyes which Laura declared to be so 'alive with expression' but had struck Bess as rather flat and black—had been drawn to their pew on more than one occasion during the service. "But, Miss Foster, you really ought to be paying attention to other things than how someone sounds and speaks and looks. At church your mind is supposed to be given over to God. You—" But she did not get the chance to instruct Laura further, for at that moment they heard someone call from behind them,

"Miss Foster!"

The voice was unmistakable. Bess watched as pink flooded the other girl's cheeks. The minister had actually run from the church door to catch up with them. He clasped Laura's proffered hand and then turned his eyes on Bess. "I don't believe we have been introduced, Miss—"

"This is my governess, Elizabeth Lanyard," Laura said, and Bess curtsied. "Miss Lanyard, this is our curate, Mr—"

"Darius Newman," the curate finished, eagerly, and thrust out his hand for Bess to shake. "I have heard a great deal about your father, Miss Lanyard, and the many good works he performed in the neighbourhood when he was alive. His absence seems most certainly to be felt."

"It certainly is, Mr Newman," Bess agreed, with quiet solemnity.

"But Mr Newman, your sermon was so very powerful," Laura gushed, and the minister's eyes returned to her, lingering on her smile for a moment before he replied,

"You are very kind to say so, Miss Foster. And—if I may ask—what do *you* think of the parable of the vineyard?"

"I think—" Laura began, and then stopped, in sudden confusion. Her cheeks went pinker still, and her eyes sought out Bess in mute appeal. "I think it is… very…"

"We were both saying, when you joined us, Mr Newman," Bess interjected, "that its moral is one that can be difficult to swallow."

"Difficult to swallow? And why is that, Miss Lanyard?"

"Well, the workers who came late to the vineyard are paid the same as those who came early—just as in the parable of the prodigal son, where the son who was wayward and absent is rewarded by his father, while his brother, who was loyal and steadfast, feels taken for granted. But I would say that the challenge presented to us by such parables is that of…" Bess paused, feeling the eyes of both Mr Newman and Laura on her, and her face began to warm.

"Yes, Miss Lanyard?" Mr Newman prompted after a moment.

"… of overcoming our own jealousy," Bess finished. "Our jealousy of those whom we consider to be reaping the rewards of our own hard labour. When we indulge in—such feelings—we are pretending that their struggles are the same as our own. We are ignoring that it is always a great cause for celebration, when one is converted to the kingdom of God, and greater still when one has been wandering and lost."

Mr Newman's eyes had been intent on Bess's face as she spoke, and now, the flicker of a smile passed over his face. "I couldn't have said it better myself, Miss Lanyard. I have always, too, been struck by the similarity between those two parables." He gazed at her for a moment more, and then, seeming to remember himself, glanced back at Miss Foster. "Do you and Miss Lanyard have a carriage?"

"No, we are walking, since it's such a fine day," declared Laura. "Will you join us, Mr Newman?"

"Nothing would give me greater pleasure, but I—" Mr Newman glanced back at the crowd still gathered outside the church doors.

"You must do your duty, of course," said Laura. "But I hope you will call on us at the Hall sometime soon?"

"Yes, I would be happy to… that is…" Mr Newman looked a little flustered by Laura's question and had to take a moment before he seemed capable of speaking again, "Well, Miss Foster—Miss Lanyard—it has been a pleasure. And now I must excuse myself."

He hurried away towards his waiting parishioners, his robes rustling around his ankles. Laura watched him go and seemed as though she would have been content to stand in the churchyard for the next hour if Bess had not hurried her on.

"I suppose you think I was too forward with him," Laura said, after they had been walking for a few minutes in silence. There was a strange quality to her tone which Bess had never heard before. "Inviting him to the Hall, I mean. But Father and I see so little of company these days."

"No, indeed, Miss Foster, I quite understand. And whenever he does call, I'm sure I would be very glad to talk to him—"

"Of course, Father and I wouldn't expect *you* to talk to any of our guests," Laura interrupted. "Not when you have such a great deal of other things to do. So, I'm sure, when Mr Newman *does* call, there will be no obligation for you to be present."

"Of course," Bess echoed after a moment, feeling that she had missed something somewhere.

"But it *was* kind of him to show such attention to you, wasn't it? And not just as my governess, but talking of your father, too, and all those other things."

"Yes," Bess agreed, feeling Laura's keen grey eyes on her as she spoke. "Very kind." They were approaching the turn-off for the road that led to the parsonage, and she gestured in that direction. "Well, I will leave you here, Miss Foster, to go visit my mother. I will be back at the Hall in time for tea."

"Good afternoon," said Laura, crisply, with a cursory glance in Bess's direction before she continued on towards the Hall. Bess watched her figure until it disappeared around the bend in the lane, and thought to herself that she must be mistaken. Surely Laura Foster could not be annoyed that Mr Newman had singled Bess out for notice! How could such a thing bother her, when it must have been clear, with the two of them standing side-by-side, which one was the beauty and which one was clumsy and plain? When Laura Foster was within sight, how could Mr Newman, or any man, prefer another? His talking to Bess had been just for the reasons Laura herself had said: it had been a kindness, a courtesy that had more to do with his admiration for her late father than anything else. Could Laura not see that?

AN UNEXPECTED VISITOR

Bess's weekly visits to her mother had at first been for her own comfort, but they soon became a necessity for other reasons. Mary Lanyard, though she had rallied again, had never really recovered from the fit of nervous exhaustion that had followed her husband's death. The recent bout of cold weather, unusual to see so early in autumn, worsened matters.

Soon Bess was not going home for her Sunday dinner anymore, but rather bringing Sunday dinner *to* her mother, in a meal usually cobbled together from whatever she could gather at the Hall. Laura urged her to take whatever she needed from the larder, and "never mind Cook." Mrs Lanyard didn't often have much appetite, but Bess would urge her to eat whatever she could and would stay until she had satisfied herself on that count. As such, her visits grew longer and longer, so that more than once, by the time she got back to Ashford Hall, the dark of night would have fully descended over the roof and treetops.

This had been going on for a few weeks when, one Sunday afternoon, Mr Newman showed up at the parsonage. Mrs Lanyard was feeling better than usual that day, strong enough to sit up with a shawl around her shoulders in the drawing room, and though she could not stand to greet her guest, she was more than able to carry on a conversation with him. Bess, seated in a chair close to her mother's side, could do nothing more than stare for the first few minutes of polite intercourse. A few hours ago, as she and Miss Foster had been coming out of church, Mr Newman had caught up with them to commiserate with Bess on her mother's illness, but she had never dreamed that he would actually come all the way to the parsonage to pay his respects.

"My daughter has told me quite a bit about you," Mrs Lanyard said, once the curate had been settled in his own chair—though 'settled' was perhaps not the best way of putting it, for he sat right at the very edge, with his long legs at a wide angle and his torso thrust forward, his elbows resting on his knees.

"Has she, indeed?" said Mr Newman, twisting around to look at Bess, who smiled back, uncertainly. "Good things, I hope."

"She says that you give very interesting sermons. I only wish I could hear one of them myself, but the walk to

Ashford church is too much for me now." There was a finality in her mother's tone which made Bess cast her eyes down to the floor. Mr Newman was silent a moment.

"We don't know what the future holds," he said at length, "and, in the meantime, Mrs Lanyard, I am at your disposal, to answer any questions you might have or to join in any discussions that might arise—every Sunday, if you like."

Mrs Lanyard, smiling, looked a little overcome by the kindness. Seeing this, Bess spoke up.

"We have no wish to take you away from your other duties, Mr Newman."

"You are very good," the curate responded, glancing at her, "but mistaken, if I may say so, Miss Lanyard, in supposing my visit here to be a duty." Returning his gaze to Mrs Lanyard, he pursued, "I have had the chance, more than once after a sermon, to speak to your daughter, and I must say that I have been impressed by her superior understanding. Knowing from where it must proceed…"

"Her father," supplied Mrs Lanyard.

"… and yourself, too, I would say, madam," Mr Newman went on, "I have been, naturally, eager to make your acquaintance."

Mrs Lanyard, smiling again, disclaimed, and as Mr Newman took out his Bible, they proceeded to discuss the particular letter of St Paul that had formed the reading at that day's service. Bess listened, mostly silent, and from time to time found her attention drifting from where it ought to have been: she watched the quiet reverence with which Mr Newman greeted each remark of her mother's, even if he did not agree with it; she noticed how he never interrupted her, even when it seemed that she had left some thought or assertion unfinished; she saw how his eyes would often turn to Bess during the conversation, silently inviting her to join in, and how they crinkled at the corners on those rare occasions when she did, as though nothing on earth could have pleased him more than her contributing.

Mr Newman stayed just over an hour and left at least one of the ladies improved; Mrs Lanyard stayed sitting up for the rest of the afternoon, and, later, finished a great part of her dinner.

Bess, for her part, was not so sure that *she* had been improved by the visit. She felt flustered whenever she thought of any one of Mr Newman's numerous attentions to her, and ashamed of her own inattention for the greater part of what had evidently been a very interesting discussion. Had she not chided Miss Foster for the very same thing in church, a few weeks ago? And here she was now, letting her own vanity distract her from the more important questions of life.

Bess had never before thought of herself as having enough vanity that she might ever be in danger of being ruled by it. But now, feeling herself all aflutter, feeling the strange and frequent urge to smile whenever she thought back on the visit, and feeling her spirits soar with one particular remark of her mother's, she knew that she ought to be on guard. The remark in question was: "You ought to buy a new dress as soon as you get your wages for the month, Bess. It's not right for you to be going around in my old hand-me-downs—and you're not the clumsy girl you once were, you know."

"Who on earth should I buy a new dress for, Mother?" Bess couldn't resist asking. "I'm sure the Fosters don't mind what I wear."

"The Fosters, perhaps not, but..." Mrs Lanyard didn't finish her sentence. "Well, your father, if he was still alive, would have wanted you to present yourself well to the world. Take my advice and buy a new dress."

THE RIVAL

Bess did take her mother's advice and was rewarded for her efforts the following Sunday by an indirect compliment from Mr Newman. Surveying her blue gown as he came up to greet her outside church, he remarked that it was pleasant to see "some colour among the congregation" and then turned his attention to Miss Foster, who was staring between them as though she couldn't believe what she was seeing.

"And how do you do, Miss Foster? What did you think of the sermon?"

"It was wonderful, just as always, Mr Newman," said Laura, quietly but firmly—she was evidently not going to be caught making the same mistake as she had before, in showing her ignorance. Mr Newman gave a funny kind of smile, which Bess could not quite read, and gestured towards the church door.

"Well, I must go back. But I may see you later, Miss Lanyard, if you will permit me to call on you and your mother again?"

There was a brief, shocked silence. Bess bowed her head and said, "Of course we would be very glad to see you, if you have the time, Mr Newman."

The minister smiled at her in parting and bowed to Laura.

"'Again'?" repeated Laura, as soon as they were out of earshot of the church. "What did he mean, call on you and your mother 'again'?"

"He means, Miss Foster, that he called on us before."

"When? Last Sunday? Why didn't you mention anything?"

Bess thought back over the last week, over day after day of mostly fruitless lessons, wrangling with Laura, negotiating with servants, bumping into Mr Foster in the hallways. "I suppose I had forgotten." This wasn't really true, as during one of these hallway encounters, she had, in fact, managed to get permission from her employer to take Wednesday afternoon off, in order to go into town and buy the gown that she was now wearing. But apart from surveying her reflection in the looking-glass when she got home, and observing that the blue went pretty well with her black hair, she had not allowed herself to give way to her own vanity, and certainly had not counted on Mr Newman coming to call on the parsonage again.

Laura gave a disbelieving shake of the head but did not question Bess any further on last Sunday. Instead, as they walked along, she suggested that Bess accompany her back to the Hall.

"But you know that I must call on my mother, Miss Foster."

"I know, of course. And I was thinking that I have been remiss in not calling on her myself, before now."

"I'm sure it wasn't expected," Bess told her. "You have been very kind, Miss Foster..."

"In giving you food and so on, but that hardly signifies, does it, especially since Father and I have more than we need?" Laura turned towards her governess in sudden decision. "I'd like to go with you today to your mother's. If you walk with me to the Hall, we can take the carriage to the parsonage. And back again. It would save you a few miles' walk; you can hardly say no to that, can you?"

Bess admitted that she could not, though she suspected that her pupil's new resolve stemmed from something other than good-will to herself or to Mrs Lanyard. Laura, satisfied, chattered happily all the way back to the house.

When they got in, she ran upstairs to make some adjustments to her toilette and re-emerged a quarter of an hour later. She had swapped her white shawl for a blue one and changed her hair so that some of the ringlets were pinned back, with the apparent design of making herself look more mature. She had not succeeded in this, at least in Bess's opinion, as with her face flushed and her eyes shining, she looked younger than ever. Divided between annoyance and sympathy, Bess watched her pupil descend the stairs, and, as they were walking out to the carriage, saw fit to deliver a gentle reminder,

"My mother has been going up and down in recent weeks, you know, Miss Foster. I am not sure how we will find her today. If she is poorly—"

"Oh, yes of course," said Laura, at once becoming more sombre in her countenance. "Don't worry on my account, Miss Lanyard. I have seen sickbeds before."

Silence followed this, as Bess had not missed the oblique reference to Mrs Foster's illness and knew better than to pursue the subject any further. It was some minutes before Laura resumed her happy chatter of before, and some minutes more before a smile crossed her face again —this on seeing Mr Newman's horse hitched to the post outside the parsonage.

"I declare, he has beaten us to it, Miss Lanyard! How surprised he will be when he sees the carriage!"

AN EARLY DEPARTURE

Mr Newman was not the only surprised one. Mrs Lanyard, who was sitting up in the drawing room again, gave a start when she saw Laura coming in with Bess. "Why, Miss Foster, how grown-up you are become! And how beautiful, too!"

"Thank you, Mrs Lanyard," said Laura, blushing more deeply and becoming, in consequence, more beautiful still. She turned to address Mr Newman. "Mrs Lanyard used to instruct me and some other girls on the Bible." Her voice took on a lofty quality. "But we were very young then, of course."

"Indeed," said Mr Newman, with a frown. He was looking towards Laura but not quite at her, with the air of one who had been suddenly confronted with the sun's glare. "Well—I am sure you could not have asked for a better instructress." As Bess took her usual seat by her mother,

Mr Newman appeared to deliberate for a moment or two —the couch where he had been sitting now being also occupied by Laura. Finally, he sat, as far from her as it was possible to get and picked up the Bible that was resting on the armrest. "Will I... continue with the psalms, Mrs Lanyard, or...?"

"Oh, don't let us interrupt!" exclaimed Laura, and Mr Newman bowed his head in acknowledgement, before opening the Bible at a marked page and tracing with his finger the numbers until he got to the psalm in question. As he began to read out loud, the three ladies listened in silence.

But the silence, while it was respectful, was not exactly attentive. This was for several reasons. On Bess's part, it was solicitude for her mother which drew her attention away from Mr Newman's reading more than once, to note any signs of exhaustion or illness that might be written on her mother's face. Mrs Lanyard herself seemed distracted by Laura's frequent movements, for the girl could hardly keep still; she kept fidgeting with her hair, fussily arranging her skirts, and then looking towards Mr Newman as though for his reaction.

Mr Newman's gaze remained resolutely fixed on his Bible, but his confusion did show a few times, in his stammering over a word here and there, or even once, when some movement of Laura's brought the edge of her skirts in contact with his trousered leg, losing his place altogether.

Bess wondered if the others, like her, felt the succeeding hour to have been the longest in their lives. She was pretty sure that Laura did not, if the latter's disappointment on the sound of approaching carriage wheels was any indication. "Already!" she exclaimed, jerking around to look out the window. "But I told Alfred not to come back for us until four, at least."

"It *is* four, Miss Foster," said Mrs Lanyard, with an indulgent smile, as she nodded towards the mantel clock.

"Is it? Well, I declare! Miss Lanyard, we shall have to take our leave."

Bess explained to Laura that she meant to stay with her mother a few hours longer and would therefore walk back to the Hall. Laura, now standing, received this news with a pout. "But I meant to save you the walk!"

"It's far too early for me to go, Miss Foster," Bess said wearily.

"Then you must let me know next time when I should order the carriage for. Well, Mrs Lanyard, I *do* hope you feel better soon!"

Mr Newman sprang into action to attend Laura out to her carriage. When the two had left, Mrs Lanyard raised her eyebrows at Bess.

"Well. I see that she means to make these visits a regular fixture?"

"She means to," said Bess, with a wry smile. "Whether she will stick to her intention or not is quite another matter."

"Oh, I think she will." Mrs Lanyard looked towards the window, though from her spot in the room, there was nothing visible except a wide expanse of slate-grey sky. "When there is a gentleman in the question..."

"Mother," Bess chided.

"Well, why shouldn't I say it? It's plain as day. She has set her sights on him, and she will turn his head if you're not careful, Bess."

"It's nothing to me if she does."

"Come now." Mrs Lanyard shifted forward in her seat with a creak. Bess, out of annoyance, had averted her gaze. Lowering her voice, her mother went on, "Bess, I have known that little girl since she was small, and her parents spoiled her beyond reason. She has never asked for anything she was not given. And now, she has seen that this man, this very fine gentleman, is paying attention to *you*, and she can't bear it. That's all. You may shake your head all you like, but it's the truth."

"She would be very foolish to think of me as a rival," said Bess, after a moment, "if indeed she does, because Mr Newman's attentions to me are nothing."

"So you say, my dear. But you will allow me the benefit of experience and age in making my own observations. *And* you will allow me to say that if you can prevent her from coming next Sunday, it would be better for everyone."

Hearing Mr Newman's footsteps in the passage, Mrs Lanyard went no further. He came back in flushed and panting hard, and seemed, for a minute or two, unable to look either of them in the eye.

"Mr Newman," said Mrs Lanyard, breaking the silence at last. "Are you quite well?"

He looked up at her and nodded at once. "Oh yes, quite well. There was just a—a puddle outside the carriage door which Miss Foster required me to lift her over, as she did not wish to get her shoes muddy. I am a little over-exerted, that is all." But Bess noticed that his hands, as he lifted up the Bible, were trembling a little, and even as they began to converse, it was some time before his breathing slowed to a regular pace.

A HIDDEN PRIZE

Not a day went by when Bess did not think of Tom Steele, at least once.

He had been her first friend, after all, and he had also formed her impressions in other directions. She still automatically compared every young man she met to him—the comparison was usually favourable to Tom, and unfavourable to everyone else.

But not long after Mr Newman had started paying attention to Bess, she found that Tom was in her mind more frequently than ever, and the comparisons that naturally arose from this, between Tom and Mr Newman, had a surprising result.

More often than not, Mr Newman emerged as superior. The first point in his favour was, of course, that he was here and Tom was not. But then there were his kindness and respect to Bess's mother, his esteem for the memory of Bess's father, and his compliments to Bess herself, not just in continuing to seek out her company, but in always seeming interested, when they were together, in what she had to say, and in noticing if she had made some change to her appearance, or if she seemed out of humour. Then there was the fact, too, that he was greatly admired by everyone, a fact which, while Bess had been taught not to value such things, still impressed itself upon her young mind.

Bess was not just surprised at the substance of the conclusion that she soon reached—that she had found a young man superior to Tom Steele—but also by how calmly she had come to it. She did not lie awake at night tormenting herself with mental back-and-forths.

The matter came to her mind only a few times a day, whenever she had a moment to herself, after Laura's lesson or when she was eating dinner in the schoolroom (Bess always dined there, while Laura and her father dined downstairs). It might make her smile or frown, depending on her mood at the time, but it seldom made her agitated.

She had decided that she liked Mr Newman better than any other young men in her acquaintance; the fact that she still did not know his feelings towards her did not put her in suspense. She felt perfectly capable of waiting until things became clearer, either through Mr Newman himself choosing to speak to her, or through his attentions to her gradually ceasing (the latter scenario seemed, to Bess, far more likely than the first).

Laura, by contrast, seemed to get more and more distracted by the day. She had, before, been a difficult pupil to manage; now she was almost impossible. All she talked about was Mr Newman. Bess had received a minute account of Laura's sensations when Mr Newman had carried her over the puddle—or "taken her in his manly arms" as Laura put it, in a phrase that seemed to have been lifted right from a sentimental novel.

As if that were not enough, each time that Laura and Mr Newman interacted subsequent to that day, Bess would be sure to receive a detailed account of everything that had been said and done—and even the *looks* that had been given—after the fact. There were not just the Sunday meetings at the parsonage, which continued, in spite of what Mrs Lanyard might have wished; there were conversations outside the church, encounters at the post office, visits to the Hall, and even the occasional sighting at a party or ball. Mr Newman seemed to be everywhere, and Laura soon wanted to be everywhere, too, to be within a chance of a glimpse of him. It was all Bess could do to keep her to the schoolroom in the mornings; afternoons she gave up as a lost cause.

If Bess had been in love with Mr Newman, as she sometimes thought herself to be, it would have been very painful to have to listen to Laura during these times. But Bess had never been able to see any of the expression in the minister's eyes that Laura talked about and could only listen with incomprehension as Laura waxed lyrical about a certain brown curl that always fell over Mr Newman's forehead whenever he bowed his head to read something out. She realised that she had never noticed Mr Newman's hair, had never even noticed its colour, except to determine that it was not as fair as Tom Steele's.

All of these one-sided conversations at least achieved the purpose of showing Bess that her mother had been mistaken about Laura. Laura was not pursuing Mr Newman for the sake of it, or because she thought him to have a preference for Bess. Her spirits were in such a state of constant flutter because she honestly believed herself to be in love with him, and, through a combination of significant looks and loaded words and accidental touches, believed it a decided thing that *he* must be falling in love with her, too.

Bess was less sure. She could see that there was something between them, but on Laura's part it seemed to be mostly happy agitation, and on Mr Newman's part, mostly discomfort.

There were times, sitting in the drawing room in the parsonage, when Laura's proximity seemed to physically pain him. He would frown deeply and hold himself as far away from her as possible, tense as a coiled spring. Once, when Laura was asked to play piano to amuse Mrs Lanyard, Mr Newman actually squeezed his eyes shut. Bess, who took some pride in the fact that her pupil played and sang rather well—it was one of the few things that she had been able to teach Laura, thus far—couldn't help feeling rather indignant on this occasion.

There was just one action of Mr Newman's which made Bess wonder if something else might lie beneath his visible discomfort in Laura's presence. It occurred after one of their afternoons at the parsonage. Laura had ordered the carriage later, so as to give Bess more time with her mother, and Mr Newman stayed long enough to be at hand to help them in. He assisted Bess first, in a very friendly and courteous way, and afterwards attended Laura, with every appearance of reluctance, holding her hand only as long as was strictly necessary until she had found her seat. But as the carriage rolled away, some instinct prompted Bess to look back through the window, and she saw Mr Newman hastily putting something in his pocket.

It wasn't until they were back at the Hall that Laura discovered she was missing one of her gloves. As it was a mild day, she had not chosen to wear them, and concluded that the missing one must have fallen somewhere. In some alarm, she sent one of the footmen back to search for it in the carriage. Bess did not tell her pupil that such a search was entirely in vain, as she was almost entirely sure of the location of Laura's glove at that moment—and she was *entirely* sure that to give Laura a hint of what she suspected would throw her into a state of helpless agitation once more. Of late, Laura's spirits had begun to calm, and she had even begun to pay attention to her studies. Her newfound enthusiasm for studying her Bible was evidently just to have something to talk about with Mr Newman, but Bess took it as a hopeful sign, nonetheless. Laura would be sixteen soon, after all. Perhaps she was finally learning the lessons that Bess had had to learn too young and moving from a silly child into a sensible woman. As for Mr Newman's unexplainable behaviour, Bess did her best to put it out of her head.

RUMOURS

The weekly visits at the parsonage had not gone unnoticed by the neighbourhood. Mr Newman, since his arrival at Ashford, had provoked great interest, being both handsome and promising, and the question of whom he might marry was of greater interest still. But as winter set in, the name that was frequently joined to his own was not that of Laura Foster, who was considered far too pretty and rich to be thrown away on a lowly curate; Bess Lanyard seemed the obvious choice.

Bess had never set much stock in what the townspeople thought of her. Her painful experiences at the hands of some of the children there, most of whom were now grown up and working in or around the town, had not been forgotten.

Laura's reaction, on the other hand, to this new spate of rumours, was one of anger and disbelief. It was, Bess imagined, an uncomfortable reminder of what was expected of her, and for a little while Laura ceased to talk of Mr Newman altogether. She took to avoiding town whenever she could. Church every Sunday became an ordeal for her, as she would be sure of hearing something there to upset her. Bess got used to the sight of her pupil in the pew next to her, clutching her hymnbook so tightly that her nails made little impressions on the cover, her mouth set in a thin line and her eyes fixed resolutely forward, even as whispers swept the church around them.

"Miss Lanyard," Laura said one afternoon after their lessons had finished and they were sewing together. It was a cold day, and the maid had built the fire in the schoolroom strong. They were sitting as close to it as it was possible to get without their skin drying out completely.

"Yes?" Bess was netting a purse, which was particularly delicate work, and tried to hide her annoyance at being interrupted.

"You don't… like Mr Newman, do you?"

Bess drew her needle up, the point gleaming as it reflected the firelight, and paused. "Of course, I like him." She heard Laura's quick intake of breath. "He is pious and courteous, and very interesting to talk to. He has done a great deal for my mother and for this neighbourhood…"

"Yes, but what about *him*? Not the things he's done or how he presents himself, but *him*! Please answer me, Miss Lanyard."

Bess looked up at last, and met her pupil's wide, pleading eyes. "I can't answer if I don't understand the question," she said, gently. "What do you want me to say, Laura? Those 'things' that you dismiss matter a great deal to me. A person's actions, indeed..."

"I didn't ask for a sermon." Laura threw down the chair-cover that she had been embroidering and stormed to the window, glaring out at the bare trees.

"Laura..."

"It's 'Miss Foster' to you."

"Miss Foster, then," Bess said. "At present, the rumours that you have heard are just that: rumours."

"'At present,'" Laura repeated, with a toss of her head. "Of course, it would be more sensible of him to marry *you*. You're a clergyman's daughter: I'm sure you would make him a better wife than I ever could. I'm too silly, and careless, and even when I try to be good it never seems to be in the right way, or for the right reasons—"

"Miss Foster, this is not the kind of talk that I like at all." Bess got to her feet, drawing herself up to her full height, though Laura, who still had her back to her, got none of the benefit of it. "You're getting carried away. Instead of worrying about what strangers think of you, and devoting so much thought to Mr Newman—worthy as he may be—why not use this time to…"

"… to think about myself," Laura finished. "Yes, you're quite right, Miss Lanyard. I've been shut up in this house for the past six months, after all. It's time I had a little variety."

"That isn't quite what I meant…"

"I've decided I'm going to visit my cousins in Manchester," Laura continued, turning around to face Bess. "They've been writing to me for months and months telling me to come. They've been having such a marvellous time, with balls and concerts. I kept saying no, that I ought to stay with Father. But I think it's clear by now that whether I stay or go makes very little difference to him, wouldn't you agree?"

Bess was silent, as she could not disagree without uttering a falsehood. For the past fortnight, she had scarcely seen Mr Foster at all.

"And I doubt Mr Newman will miss me either." The bitterness in Laura's voice was unmistakable. "So, I intend to go, and enjoy myself."

"And what am I to do, Miss Foster, while you are gone?" Bess asked, after a moment's pause.

"Oh, you may stay here if you wish. I'm sure Father and the servants will have no objection. And I'm sure you can find *plenty* of things to occupy yourself with. All those books that you read, that you are so fond of discussing with Mr Newman." Laura turned, and began to move for the door, her skirts rustling.

"How long will you be gone?" Bess asked quietly.

"I don't know—two weeks, maybe three. It all depends on how much fun I'm having!" Laura gave a laugh which sounded harsh and forced. "I'll write to you once I get there and tell you. Now I'd better go pack."

For the rest of the day, Bess did not see Laura at all, and she awoke the next morning to find that her pupil had already left to get the early train from Bradford.

THE INVITATION

The day of Laura's departure was a Saturday, and upon reflection, Bess deemed it wiser to wait until her visit the following day to tell her mother what had happened. After that, she planned to stay at the parsonage until such a time as Laura returned from Manchester.

Probably the visit to her cousins would be shorter than she had said it would be—probably, after she felt that she had made her point, Laura would return to Ashford. Bess felt that she was right in supposing this, given Laura's relentless pursuit of Mr Newman up until now.

Or maybe it would have been more accurate to say that Bess *hoped* she was right, because her future, and her mother's, depended on it.

However inattentive Edward Foster might be in general, Bess knew that he would not keep her on indefinitely and continue to pay her simply for living in his house. So, Laura would have to return, and soon.

Bess spent much of that Saturday in moody abstraction, huddled close to the schoolroom fire. She tried, more than once, to pick up one of those books that Laura had mockingly referred to but found that she could not focus on the words. Her thoughts kept returning to Laura, as she wondered what kind of reception her pupil would be enjoying in Manchester.

As the sky over Ashford Hall turned dark, Bess wondered if Laura was looking out at the city lights at that moment, wishing herself back among her friends. Or was she bustling off to some assembly room, full of excitement and eagerness, ready to make several young men fall in love with her so that she might forget the only one who would not? Bess suddenly felt a strange constriction in her chest as she thought of her pupil. How could it be that she was missing her already, when her presence was so tiresome and her feelings so large and lavish that they oppressed everyone else's?

At the opening of the schoolroom door, Bess looked up, ready to thank the maidservant for bringing her dinner tray. She instead saw Mr Foster, who cast his eye over the furnishings over the schoolroom as though they were unfamiliar to him and told Bess in an offhand way that she could join him for dinner that evening if she liked.

"Make whatever changes are necessary," he said, waving a hand at her plaid work gown, "And be ready in half an hour. I can send one of the maids up to help you, if you like."

It took Bess a moment to understand what he meant. "No, no, sir," she stammered. "I can dress myself—that is, I don't need a maid to—thank you."

Mr Foster gave a funny sort of half-smile, that was not really a smile at all, and turned and left.

POOR

Bess practically tripped over her own skirts in her haste to get upstairs. In her small room, which was just off the servants' quarters, she unearthed every dress from her wardrobe and laid them out on her bed. There were only three besides the one she was wearing now: the new blue one, which was not really suitable for the evening, a black stuff gown that was even worse, and a moss green silk that had been her mother's before.

Thinking again of how Mr Foster had offered to send her a maid, Bess shook her head in disbelief. What a stir that would have made downstairs, if she had accepted! And how the maid would have made everyone in the servants' hall laugh, telling them about Miss Lanyard's poor wardrobe! Bess settled on the green silk, though it was a little tight around the arms, and left her hair in two dark loops around her ears, just as she always wore it. She left her room with five minutes to spare and was making her stiff way down the main stairs when a thought struck her and made her pause.

What if this dinner invitation by Mr Foster was just a precursor for his dismissal of Bess? Was this just his way of apologising for his daughter's impulsiveness in leaving Ashford, throwing herself on the care of her cousins, and thus rendering a governess redundant? Wherever she went looking for work next, her potential employers were not going to look kindly on the fact that she had barely lasted two months in her previous two situations.

Suddenly Bess was in no hurry to get downstairs.

A NEW NAMELESS FEAR

Mr Foster was waiting for her outside the dining room when she arrived. "No doubt you have heard, Miss Lanyard, that a fine lady is expected to keep a gentleman waiting," he said as he came forward, "But for mealtimes in this house, we always keep to the hour."

"I'm sorry," Bess said, without really meaning it—without really feeling anything at all apart from blind panic. As Mr Foster took her arm to lead her into the dining room, she hoped he would not feel her shaking.

They sat at opposite ends of a long table, and Bess felt the servants move around her like a dark blur; she heard them murmuring beyond the circle of candlelight. She scarcely knew which knife and fork to use, or whether to put her napkin on her lap or leave it folded on the table. When the soup had been poured, Bess raised a spoonful to her mouth at once, and nearly scalded her tongue.

"Why do you look so pale, Miss Lanyard?" asked Mr Foster, as she was still wincing from the shock. He had been watching her all the while and didn't seem to have touched his own soup. "Is it because I was so stern about your being late?"

"No, sir," Bess said after a moment, and raised another spoonful to her lips, blowing on it discreetly before she swallowed.

"I must say, you are looking very well," Mr Foster continued, and Bess's spoon froze in midair. "I have never seen you in that dress before."

"It's for… special occasions, sir," Bess said, replacing the spoon in the bowl; with his eyes still on her, she was suddenly feeling too self-conscious to eat.

"So, you consider dining with me a special occasion? Well, well, that is quite flattering." Out of the corner of her eye, Bess saw Mr Foster finish his glass of wine, and gesture to one of the servants to pour him another.

Deciding that she could not bear the suspense any longer, Bess burst out, "I don't know why Miss Foster has gone to Manchester, sir."

"Nor do I," said Mr Foster, calmly, peering into his now full glass of wine. He raised it to his lips, and half of the contents disappeared in one gulp. "That girl's reasons are unfathomable to me. But she was fixed on going when she came to talk to me yesterday, so I let her go."

"I'm sure she will be back soon," said Bess, a little desperately.

"Are you?" Mr Foster returned his gaze to her. "*I'm* not. But let's not concern ourselves with her now. She has gone to her cousin's to enjoy herself, apparently; let's pretend to believe that is true."

"But, sir," Bess said after a moment's pause. "Isn't that why you—isn't that why I'm—"

"Hmm?"

Bess leaned back as one of the servants came to clear away her soup bowl. She waited until Mr Foster's had been cleared too before saying, faintly, "With Miss Foster gone, sir—does that mean that I'm…"

"Oh, of course not. Is *that* what has you looking so pale? James, pour her some more wine."

"I don't need any more wine, thank you," said Bess quickly. She had not touched her own glass yet.

"James," said Mr Foster again, and the footman came forward, filling Bess's glass until it was almost overflowing. She looked at it warily.

"Drink," said Mr Foster, and Bess slowly raised the glass to her lips. She took a small sip. "Come, Miss Lanyard, a little bit more than that." Bess took another sip and put down the glass again. She felt a light swirling sensation inside her, which was unfamiliar but not entirely unpleasant.

"That's much better," declared her master. "Why, you have a little more colour in your cheeks already."

Bess put down her glass and forced herself to meet Mr Foster's gaze. "So, sir, am I..."

"You are welcome to stay here for as long as you like."

"But my wages..."

"Will be paid, of course, even in my daughter's absence. It is only fair, is it not? I engaged you as my daughter's governess, and it is merely her absence that is preventing you from doing your duty."

Bess nodded slowly. "Thank you, sir." This was good news, she reminded herself. This was an end to the anxiety that had been tormenting her all day.

But as the servants came in with their main course and moved up and down the table with serving dishes, a whole host of new, nameless fears swooped in. Bess told herself that she was just being silly. She was just imagining the intent look in Mr Foster's eyes every time she chanced a glance up at him. And when he urged her, once and twice more, to drink her wine, he was just being solicitous for her enjoyment of the meal. Since he drank a great deal, he naturally expected his guests to do so, too. Bess therefore took a small sip every time he told her to, out of politeness.

SLEEPLESS

W hen dessert had been served and cleared, the servants filed out of the room. As the baize door closed behind the last one, Bess made to get out of her chair, but was stilled by a motion of Mr Foster's hand. "Not just yet, Miss Lanyard." She watched as he got up himself and walked to the sideboard. He came back with a bottle in his hand, and seizing hold of the chair with the other, picked it up and dragged it down the length of the table, until he had come to Bess's side. Placing the bottle on the table between them, he sat in his chair with a sigh of satisfaction, and said, "Now we may talk properly. Will you have some port, Miss Lanyard?"

Bess shook her head apologetically. "After the wine, sir, I don't think…"

"Yes, I suppose you're not used to it," Mr Foster said, glancing up at her with an expression that was almost kind. "Well, I will, in any case." He poured himself a glass and took a generous swallow. Then, wiping his mouth with his napkin, he leaned back in his chair and said, "Is it true that you are engaged to the curate?"

Bess, caught off guard, looked at him blankly. "Mr Newman," he prompted. "Is it true, Miss Lanyard?"

"No, sir," Bess said fervently. "It's not true."

"I thought not. I imagined you would not be so keen to keep your position here, otherwise." Mr Foster took another sip of his port. "But he has been paying attention to you, I hear?"

Bess was silent.

"That is what they have been saying in the town, in any case, and I have even heard it from a few of the servants, too." Mr Foster nodded towards the closed baize door. "Ordinarily I wouldn't pay attention to such rumours, of course, but when it concerns a young woman under my employ, naturally I have some interest—"

"They are just rumours, sir," said Bess, with a new firmness. Those nameless fears of dinnertime now having identified themselves in her mind, she felt some of her own natural courage returning in defiance of them. "And I would prefer if you did not mention them again."

Mr Foster looked faintly surprised. "Very well, then I won't." He reached for the bottle again. "Are you sure you won't have some port?"

"I'm sure, sir. In fact, I think I should be going now."

Bess rose from her chair. He rose with her, and they stood facing one another for a moment. Bess was a few inches taller than Mr Foster, but that did not seem to concern him; he held himself with every appearance of ease, his eyes passing over her face in a proprietary way.

"To the drawing room?" he said, after a moment's silence. "I will join you there shortly."

"No, sir," said Bess. "To bed. I am very tired."

"Very well," said Mr Foster again. "Then I will bid you goodnight."

"Goodnight, sir." Bess gave a ghost of a curtsy and turned towards the door. As she was doing so, she felt his hand move to the small of her back and rest there, just for a moment. The touch burned through the material and right onto her skin like a brand.

That night in bed, it took her hours to fall asleep; she found herself starting awake every time she heard the creak of a door, or footsteps in the passage outside. She reminded herself that there were servants sleeping in rooms nearby—just servants. But it was no use: she could not rest until she had gotten up, dragged a chair in front of her door, and climbed back into bed. Then, and only then, could she sleep easy.

DEEP WATER

Mrs Lanyard and Mr Newman were both surprised, at the parsonage the following day, when Bess showed up on foot without Laura. They were more surprised still when they heard about where the young lady had gone.

"You mean to tell me she went gallivanting off to Manchester, without so much as an explanation?" Mrs Lanyard demanded. "I wonder that her father can allow it."

"I imagine that the countryside must get dull, for a young lady of Miss Foster's disposition," said Mr Newman. He spoke as though choosing his words very carefully. "Perhaps Mr Foster had the wisdom to recognise that."

"But what about Bess? What is she to do in the meantime? She might have invited you to go with her, at least."

"I would have said no if she had. I have no desire to go to Manchester, or to leave you," said Bess, frankly, and her mother glanced at her with a startled smile. "And as for my position, I think it is still safe. Mr Foster has assured me that I will still be paid the same amount."

"Well, then." Mrs Lanyard deliberated a moment. "Well, it's all rather strange, but I suppose you ought to stay in the Hall and make yourself useful in whatever way you can, until Miss Foster returns."

This was what Bess had been afraid that her mother would say. "I was thinking I might come and stay with you."

"But what would Mr Foster think? He's been kind enough to let you stay and get the same pay even though you are not working. I think if you were to come to stay *here* while Miss Foster is gone, that would be stretching his good-will a little too far." Her mother shook her head decisively. "No, Bess, I can manage perfectly well here on my own, as long as I have a little help now and again. And I have that with you already."

"And if I may be so bold," Mr Newman added, "you have me, too, Mrs Lanyard. I am at your disposal. My duties around the parish often bring me close to this house. If Miss Lanyard has no objection, I could call on you here once or twice during the week."

"Of course, I have no objection," said Bess, still looking at her mother. "But I just…"

"Bess is very kind and good, and she always wants to manage everything, just like her father did before her," declared Mrs Lanyard, and Mr Newman made a noise of assent.

Bess looked from one to the other and wondered what they would say if she were to tell them that her wanting to stay here was out of her own self-interest rather than concern for her mother. Would they still be smiling at her like that if they knew that she had been wined and dined by Mr Foster last night, or that she had sneaked out of Ashford Hall this morning while the grass was still wet with dew, creeping through the woods like a thief and fearing, at every turn, that she would come upon *him*?

Bess did not know how they would react if she told them of her fears—whether they would blame her for any part of her own conduct that might have been encouraging to Mr Foster, or put all blame on his shoulders. But she did know that her mother was right about at least one thing. If Bess stayed here, her chances of keeping her position at Ashford Hall were lower than they would be if she went back to wait for Laura there. Since her governess's wages were the only thing keeping them afloat, as her mother was now too weak to take in students the way she had done before, if Bess were to lose her position, they would find themselves in deep water.

Bess also knew that if her mother heard about how Mr Foster had behaved, she would not insist on Bess going back to the Hall. So, in the end, it was an easy choice between telling them and not telling them. One threatened her position, the other didn't.

Mr Newman stayed longer at the parsonage that day than he ever had before. He struck Bess as happier and easier than she had seen him in a long time. By this time, the three of them no longer stood on ceremony with one another; Mr Newman called them both by their Christian names, and when the time came for Bess to depart, it seemed an understood thing that Mr Newman would walk her back as far as the Hall.

PROPOSAL

I t was already dark when they left. Mr Newman kept a light hold on his horse's halter as they walked along the lane, but the creature seemed perfectly content with their slow pace, giving only a gentle whicker every now and then.

Though they were still miles away from the Hall, Bess was already seeing in her mind's eye the lighted windows of the house looming up before her, the long dark staircase that she would have to traverse to get to her quarters. She did not imagine that Mr Newman's thoughts were tending in a very different direction, until he burst out with, "This Manchester business."

Bess glanced at him in confusion. Through the semi-darkness, she saw Mr Newman glance back at her. "I mean," he said, "Miss Foster going there so suddenly. Did she really not give you an explanation?"

Bess thought back on her argument with Laura, wondering how much she could reveal without also giving away the source of it. "She said she was in need of some amusement. Her cousins have been writing to her for some time inviting her to visit. And I believe there are many concerts and balls there…" She broke off, hearing Mr Newman's dry laugh.

"It is just as I thought, then," he said. "Forgive me—I don't wish to talk ill of your pupil. I'm sure you have greatly improved her, at least as much as it is possible to improve such a creature. Of late, I thought I was beginning to notice a change in her. She seemed, if still possessed of a weak understanding, at least aware of that shortcoming, and fixed on making whatever amends for it that she could. Some of the questions that she has asked me these last few weeks, after my sermons, have even shown sufficient evidence of an inquiring mind…"

"You are mistaken, Mr Newman," said Bess after a moment, for the curate had trailed off, "if you suppose Miss Foster possessed of a weak understanding. In my view it is very strong—it is just that she often lacks the inclination to apply it when needed."

"Maybe it is not her understanding that is weak, then, but rather her resolve. I see that as almost worse. If one has the abilities, but chooses to bury them—"

"Like the servants in Matthew's gospel, burying their talents," Bess supplied, and she saw Mr Newman's smile of recognition in the semi-darkness.

"Exactly. If someone has so many gifts, so many abilities, as Miss Foster so evidently does... which anyone might see... and yet only turns them towards their own amusement or gratification..." His tone had changed now, become almost distracted, and after a moment's silence, he patted his horse's neck and resumed, in businesslike tones, "But I am forgetting my own purpose. I have been wanting, for some time, to speak to you, Miss Lanyard— Bess. And I do not know when I will get the chance again. We always seem surrounded by people. So I hope you will allow me to tell you—I hope you will allow me to ask you—"

"Mr Newman," said Bess, and he turned towards her again with a start.

"Yes?"

"I think, if I may presume to say so, I know already what you are about to ask me."

"Do you?" He sounded relieved. "Then, what is your answer?"

Bess decided the matter just as calmly as she had decided, a month before, that she ought to prefer Mr Newman to Tom Steele. "My answer is no, Mr Newman."

"'No?'" he repeated, and sunk into silence, so that for the next few minutes, the only sounds were the snorting of the horse, the tread of their feet on the gravelly lane, and the distant barking of a dog.

"Might I ask, Bess," Mr Newman said at length, "why you have not even taken the time to consider my proposal?"

"I wasn't aware that you had made one," Bess couldn't help responding.

"You're quite right, of course. Allow me to make amends now." Mr Newman came to a halt in the lane and reached for Bess's gloved hand. As he was on the point of kissing it, his horse nudged his shoulder, and Mr Newman, recoiling from the horse's sniffing nostrils, dropped Bess's hand. "Forgive me," he stammered. Bess was suddenly glad it was so dark, as she had been seized by the sudden, uncontrollable urge to laugh. As Mr Newman reached for her hand again, Bess did her best to compose her features. "Bess Lanyard, I think it must be clear—I hope it is, by now—how much I esteem and admire you. Your wit, your understanding, your virtue and your kindness cannot but strike any discerning person, and over these last few weeks, your company has become very precious to me. There is not much I can offer you, of course; you know all that I am. But if you would do me the honour of accepting my hand in marriage, I will do everything in my power to provide for you."

His speech being concluded, he held onto her hand for a moment more, peering in the direction of her face as though trying, in vain, to discern whatever expression might be on it. "Well," he prompted, without allowing for more than a half-minute of silence to pass between them. "Well, Bess, is your answer still…"

"My answer is still the same as before," Bess told him, and he let go of her hand.

"But—I don't understand. That is… I'm sure that we could make each other very happy."

"I'm not sure of that at all, Mr Newman. You do me a great honour by asking me such a thing, and by telling me so many things in my favour. Indeed, I think it is more than I deserve."

"It is *not* more than you deserve," he said, with surprising vehemence. "You are the very best of women, Bess. There is no one else whom I could imagine sharing my home and hearth, no one else who meets the struggles of life with a smile, the way you do. I feel—but I have talked enough of myself. What of *your* feelings, Bess? I have had the impression, since we met, that my company was not disagreeable to you—that my conversation was, at least, not unpleasant, but perhaps I have been mistaken too, in that…"

"I like you very much, Mr Newman, and I am very grateful for the friendship that you have shown myself and my mother. But I do not think that I like you well enough to marry you."

"Ah," said Mr Newman, with something that sounded like a wince. "Well, there is no helping that, I suppose."

They began to walk again, in painful silence. The dark shapes of the trees around Ashford Hall were soon visible ahead. Bess was on the point of telling Mr Newman that he did not have to walk her all the way to the gatehouse, especially after what had just passed between them, when he broke out with another question.

"You said—Miss Lanyard… forgive me. But you said that you did not think that we could make *each other* happy. Does that mean—that as well as not liking me well enough, you doubt whether *you* could make me happy?"

"Yes," said Bess, quietly. "In fact, I'm quite sure that I could not."

"Then you are mistaken." Mr Newman half-turned towards her, and then faced forward again. "But I have already made my feelings plain, I think, and there is nothing more I can say."

He left her at the gates, his lanky figure disappearing into the growing dark.

HORROR

B ess reflected, as she walked through the silent woods, that what he had said was true; he had, in more ways, perhaps, than he realised, made his feelings absolutely plain.

He had opened his proposal to her by talking of Miss Foster, by complaining of her unconquerable nature; he had talked of esteeming and admiring Bess, but nowhere in his speech had there been any mention of love.

Bess had no foolish notions of romance—she had had no opportunity, in her lonely childhood and premature entry into womanhood, to form them. She knew that many marriages had been built on the basis of esteem and admiration alone; perhaps her own parents' union had even arisen from such mundane feelings. But given what she had observed and now suspected, Mr Newman, while he might not love her, might very well harbour those feelings for another.

Bess tried to imagine what she might have done if Miss Foster had been out of the question—whether she would have accepted Mr Newman then. But it seemed to her that her answer would still have been the same. Why that was, she could not or would not tell; the answer was tied up with the memory of a young man with very blue eyes, whom she was not likely to see again. She wondered how on earth she was going to explain this to her mother, who, she knew, thought Mr Newman such a perfect match for her.

The square of light on the floor of the dark hall as she entered, and the sound of crackling fire from the dining room, brought Bess back to reality. She had closed the door softly behind her, and now crept forward, intending to pass to the staircase as quietly as she could. When she was about halfway there, Mr Foster's pointer came lolloping out through the open door of the dining room to greet her. He did not bark but panted very loudly and excitedly as he came up to Bess, thrusting his snout into her hand. She patted his floppy ears resignedly as Mr Foster's voice came from within,

"Who's there?"

"It's me, sir," she called back, after a moment of debating whether or not she should answer at all. "Miss Lanyard." There was a silence, and then she heard the creak of a chair and footsteps across the floor. Mr Foster appeared in the doorway. The sight of him made Bess's heart sink, not just because it was what she had been dreading all day, but because he looked rather the worse for wear. There was a hard red flush in his cheeks, his eyes were watery and bloodshot, and though he was evidently incapable of standing properly, he did not seem to notice his own body rocking back and forth. He must have started drinking hours ago, Bess thought with a flash of alarm, just as he opened his mouth to say,

"You left very early this morning."

"Yes, sir," she said, adjusting her stance slightly in a discreet attempt to put some more distance between them. "I had to go to church and visit my mother afterwards."

"How is your mother?" Mr Foster asked, but before she could reply, he went on, "You must be cold. Come and sit by the fire with me."

"I'm not cold at all, sir, but I must be getting to bed—"

"Just for a minute or two. Come." Mr Foster advanced towards her, taking hold of her shoulder and elbow as she was beginning to back away.

"Sir..."

"Miss Lanyard, don't refuse me again." This close, she could smell the spirits from him. "I am not asking for so very much, am I? Come and sit."

He half-led, half-dragged her into the dining room. The pointer trotted after them, his alert brown eyes fixed on Bess. "Here," said Mr Foster, indicating the armchair where he had just been sitting, but Bess shook her head.

"That is too close to the fire for me, sir. I would prefer to stand."

"Would you? Then I will stand, too. It is only manners, after all." He stooped to pick up his glass, where he had set it down by the armchair, and moved towards Bess, stopping only when he was a few inches away from where she was standing. "Tell me." He was swaying again, so that the liquid in his glass sloshed to and fro. "Did you meet the curate again today?"

"Yes, sir. Mr Newman gave the service."

"Are you sure you're not cold? Come a little closer to the fire."

"I am not cold, sir."

"Then why are you shaking?"

Bess had not noticed it until he said it. Then, looking down at herself, she saw her own violently trembling hands like those of a stranger. The very material of her dress was rippling with the involuntary movement of her body.

"Have some of this." Mr Foster was holding out his glass to her. "It will warm you up nicely."

"No, sir. I will not."

"I can get you your own if you would prefer."

"I would prefer to go to bed—" But Bess did not get to finish her sentence. Mr Foster, putting his glass down on the mantlepiece, so far near the edge that it seemed like the slightest tremor in the earth would knock it down, came forward and pulled Bess to him. The smell of spirits was suddenly overwhelming. Bess was only dimly aware of what was happening when Mr Foster began to kiss her; it took a minute or two for her body to respond, and when she finally pulled away to cry, "Let me go, sir, let me go!" the loud ring of her own voice through the empty dining room shocked her more than anything else had so far.

"It's no use shouting like that," Mr Foster said, pressing up close to her again. "All the servants have gone to bed. There's no one but you and me."

As he moved in to kiss her, Bess turned her head away, but one hand came to grasp her chin, jerking it back to face forward. She was taller than him, but he was stronger; his other arm had reached around her to pin her own arms to her sides, so that she could not push him away or fight back. He kissed her again, forcefully, steering her away from the fire as he did so, until her back had struck the wall. As Mr Foster pulled away to catch his breath and look at her, Bess had a sudden, trembling sense of what was coming next.

"Please, sir," she said hoarsely. Nearby, the pointer had started whining, but she could not see exactly where it was.

Mr Foster's face blurred before her as her eyes filled with tears.

Then she closed them altogether, squeezed them shut tightly as he kissed her again. She desperately imagined herself outside of this room. Anywhere but here. On her dear hill, under cover of the trees, alone and at peace. Far away from the Foster mansion...

INTERRUPTION

"Sir? Is everything all right?"

An outside voice intruded upon them.

Bess felt Mr Foster jerk in response. She had gone limp in his arms by then, unable to move, numb to the caresses of her assailant.

As he removed himself from her, turning, she saw over his shoulder that the butler was standing on the threshold in his dressing gown, holding a candle.

"Yes, everything's fine," Mr Foster snapped. "What are you doing up at this time, Andrews?"

"The dog was barking very loud, sir, and it woke a few of us up. We thought there might be an intruder; I was sent down to check." The butler's gaze strayed to Bess, and then he quickly averted it again.

Bess had not heard the dog barking; by the looks of it, Mr Foster had not, either.

"Well, as you can see, there isn't," he said, crossly. "So, you may rest easy, Andrews."

"Thank you, sir." The butler lingered in the threshold a moment more. It was not much, but it was just long enough for Bess to slip out from under the cage of Mr Foster's arms and streak across the room.

"I will go upstairs with you, Andrews," she announced, in a voice that was too loud and too bright, "As it is time for me to be going to bed, too."

"Very good, Miss Lanyard," said Andrews. Bess followed him, not daring to look back to see Mr Foster's reaction.

FITFUL SLEEP

A s they climbed the dark stairs, the candle flame flickering in its holder, Andrews was silent. It was almost as if Bess was not there. When they had reached the passage that led to the servants' quarters, she whispered, "Thank you."

"I don't know what you're referring to, Miss Lanyard," replied the butler, stiffly. His gaze strayed downwards, towards Bess's chest, for just a fraction of a second, and then he bowed and turned away.

Bess, looking down herself, saw that the bodice of her blue gown—the gown that she had been so proud of, the gown on which Mr Newman had complimented her—had been cruelly torn right across her chest, revealing the white chemise underneath. She put her hand over it and kept it there, even though she met no one else on the way to her room.

When inside, she dragged the chair in front of the door again, threw herself on the bed, and lay fully-clothed for a long time, simply staring into the darkness, silently weeping herself into a fitful sleep.

DISMISSED

The knock on her door came so early the next morning that Bess, as she sat up in bed, thought that it must still be night. Through the dim blue light of pre-dawn, she stared at the door, watching as the chair rattled under pressure from the other side. There came another knock, and then a voice, "Miss Lanyard?" Hearing that it was not Mr Foster's, she got up and wrapped a shawl around her shoulders.

"Miss Lanyard?" said one of the maids as Bess opened the door. The girl looked pale and frightened. "I'm sorry to wake you so early, but Mr Foster says you're to go at once. He told me to tell you that you are dismissed, and to pack your bags right away. He wants you to be gone by the time he gets up for his breakfast."

Bess took all this in hazily. "What time is it?"

"It's just gone six, miss."

"Six, already? But it can't be." Bess reeled back a little, and reached for the doorframe to support herself.

"Please, miss," said the maid, who was watching her anxiously. "I've never seen the master so angry before."

Bess nodded, rubbing a hand over her face. "I will be packed and ready in a quarter of an hour."

She was true to her word; she descended the stairs of Ashford Hall, valise in hand, at quarter past six, and was coming down the drive under a rapidly lightening sky when she heard footsteps crunching on the gravel behind her. Bess turned, ready to defend herself—though she knew not how—if it was Mr Foster. But it was the same maid, rushing after her with an envelope in her hand.

"Please, miss. Your wages for the first three months. The master says you are to have them."

Bess nodded and took the envelope. "Very good, thank you, Martha," she said, in a crisp, practical voice that was miles away from how she was feeling at that moment. She had been so dazed that she had not even thought to ask for her wages. Under the maid's gaze, she pocketed the envelope, and faced forward again.

"Good luck, miss," said the girl from behind her, sounding as though she was close to tears. Whatever small resistance had been left in Bess crumbled after that, and as the tears ran down her face, she clamped a hand over her own mouth, and did not make any reply.

NEW SCENES

Bess and her mother sold the parsonage in the New Year.

They did not get much for it, since most of the most valuable furniture had already been sold over the last few years, but what little they came away with was enough to enable them to rent a cottage in Ashford.

Bess disliked living in town, close to so many unpleasant scenes from her childhood, but she did not have to endure it for long: at the end of January came a letter from Mrs Huxby, who had once been Miss Baxter and was now living in Leeds. She wrote to tell them that her friend was looking for staff in a new ladies' school that she had just opened, and Mrs Huxby had recommended her former teacher. Since Bess's mother was too ill to work even from the comforts of her own home, let alone travel, it was arranged that Bess would take her place.

So, for the first time in her life, Bess Lanyard took the train from Bradford to Leeds, and watched through the window as she was whirled through the countryside. The further she drew away from home, the larger the people from home loomed in her mind. She thought of how kind Mr Newman had been, in helping herself and her mother find the place in town, and how he had never repeated his offer to Bess or put pressure on her to think again, even though she herself had had moments where she thought she might have acted rashly in rejecting him. She thought about how Laura Foster had never once called on her or written to her, even after she had returned from her visit to Manchester. She thought about how frightened the maids in Mr Foster's household had looked, and wondered whether, in the absence of herself, he might have turned his attentions to them instead.

Leeds was large and strange. Being down in its streets, Bess felt hemmed in; she could not look about her and see for miles as she did back home. The young ladies who attended the school where she worked were mostly merchants' daughters, and their talk of market days and power-looms flew over Bess's head. She knew that there were big cotton factories here, whose dominance had been well-established decades before; she passed their yards whenever she did venture around town; she saw their workers teeming through the streets. But she understood nothing about the industry.

She felt as out of place here as she would have done in London or Dublin. No one talked to her, not even the other women who taught in the school. There was no one to call on or visit. The church which she attended on Sundays was full of factory workers, who would stare quite freely at Bess during service, but sloped away if she tried to engage them in conversation.

She found herself looking forward to Thursdays, for that was the day when her weekly letter from her mother would usually arrive. Despite being confined to bed for much of the time, Mrs Lanyard seemed to pick up a good deal of news about the goings-on of town; perhaps because so many people called on her. Mr Newman visited at least twice a week. Mrs Lanyard, unaware of the fact that he had proposed to Bess (a piece of information that she had never gotten around to telling her), described him as "subdued" during these visits. "But he talks very often of you, Bess," read a postscript in one of her letters, "and is still anxious that something be done about your unfair dismissal."

Bess herself was not anxious that that matter be brought to light at all. She had repaired the tear in her gown, though the new stitching was so obvious that she only ever wore it covered with a pinafore.

When she thought back on that night, the moment that still filled her with horror was not the moment when Mr Foster had kissed her—although that had certainly been unpleasant—but the moment when the butler Andrews had seen them from the doorway. Bess hated to think of talk getting downstairs, and of certain servants misunderstanding the situation. She was sure that the maids, or at least the one who had summoned her in the morning, Martha, knew what Mr Foster really was—but did the others? She remembered how silent and stiff the butler had been with her afterwards. It seemed unfair, after her parents had taken such care to raise her to be virtuous, that all their hard work be undone by circumstances that Bess had been unable to prevent. She had been unable to overpower Mr Foster, and if Andrews had not shown up, she would have been unable to outrun him either.

Because of all this, the matter was all tied up with her own shame, and she wished more than anything else that Mr Newman and her mother would just forget about it.

She had been dismissed from her second position just the same as she had been dismissed from her first, and she had been exceptionally lucky to get anything else at all: that was it. That was the fact of which she tried to remind herself, as often as possible. So, sometimes, when the heat and noise of the schoolroom got to be too much, she would set her girls doing exercises, and go downstairs, exiting the school through the street door. She would stand for a minute or two and watch the carriages roll past, the ladies and gentlemen on foot stopping to look in shop windows, the workmen standing in doorways smoking, or walking arm-in-arm with one another during their dinner hour.

A city like this did not really suit Bess, and probably never would, but still there was something about it: a sort of spell that all that motion and colour cast upon her.

THE LETTER

Tucked away in Ashford, the movements of the outside world had been like ripples on a pond to Bess; even wars involving their own kingdom, like the one that had been going on for the last three years on the Crimean Peninsula, had seemed remote and unreal. But in a city like Leeds, with the passage of so many people in and out, news broke in with an immediacy that it had never had before; suddenly, reality was right there before Bess, impossible to ignore. For the first time, she felt as though the things that were happening elsewhere in the world were happening to real people, right then. This was especially the case one day in April, when the soldiers came home victorious from the Crimean War.

For days on end, the streets were dotted with red coats, and scabbards gleamed in the sunlight. The young ladies in Bess's school became impossible to manage; a number of them took up permanent stations by the window, and any chance encounter with the uniformed men, in shops or on the street, would be gleefully related to one another and in most cases, Bess was nearly sure, shamelessly embellished. Some of the accounts even had the officers professing love or proposing marriage to these girls on the street, and while she was fond of her pupils and rated their qualities very highly, she did not find such scenarios entirely plausible.

But certain little romances did spring up which were not just limited to the girls' imagination. A love letter or two was intercepted by one of the school mistresses, and one evening an unfortunate soldier was caught loitering in the back garden of the school, given a round telling-off by the principal, and informed that "Miss Letitia" was too busy with her studies to come down and be serenaded. After that particular incident, the staff held a meeting to determine how to deal with this new and alarming problem, and it was concluded that the girls must not be allowed out for the time being, even to attend church on Sundays.

Bess watched all these goings-on with amusement. She found her fellow teachers' overzealous guarding of their girls' virtue just as ridiculous as the fact that those same girls were so easily dazzled by a uniform. For her part, she was inclined to be a little more indulgent, and when, one afternoon, following a complicated interchange of notes, a certain unruly pupil crept out of the schoolroom, Bess pretended not to notice.

She had her own reasons for not wanting to chase after young Miss Hamilton at that moment. She had not yet had the chance to read her mother's latest letter, which had arrived yesterday, and as the girls were all working on their essay compositions, Bess at last took out the dear envelope, whose thickness informed her that many sheets of paper were waiting for her perusal. She unfolded the first sheet carefully and began to read. Bit by bit the schoolroom dissolved around her, the row of bent heads and the scratching of pens replaced by the flat sweep of countryside and the low moan of wind. She still could not picture the cottage in Ashford as home, so she saw her mother sitting at her fold-up writing desk in the drawing room of the parsonage. She imagined her mother pausing once she had related one piece of news, gazing out the window, until she had thought of the next.

Bess read of Miss Foster's coming-out, which had, apparently, been a great success so far; glowing reports were travelling from London to Ashford of the many admirers whom she had gathered and the many fashionable balls that she had attended with her cousins since the opening of the season in February, two months before. She read of Mrs Collins in town, who had bought their chickens after they had sold the parsonage, and still brought a basket of eggs for Mrs Lanyard every time she called, for which she refused to be paid. Then—the imagined scene of the parsonage wavered around Bess, reordering itself into the real one of the schoolroom, for she simply couldn't believe what she read next.

"Do you remember Mr Steele, the strange young man who stayed with us for a fortnight, the winter after your dear father died?"

Her mother wrote.

"It is nearly five years ago now. He had been carousing around the country with his friends, and got away from them somehow, injuring himself. He used to persuade you to slip him a glass of my sherry every evening— perhaps you don't remember that part, for I know you would never do such a thing now. But he was very cunning and rather charming, too."

By now, Bess's heart was throbbing in painful suspense, and as she was obliged to turn the page over to its other side, she almost tore the paper in her impatience to read what came next.

"It is the oddest thing, but he called on me recently. The vicar's wife at the parsonage had

told him where to find me, for I believe he called there first. He is very changed, Bess; he was barely more than a boy that time when he stayed with us, but now he looks very distinguished. He has been abroad, involved in the fighting. He tells me that this is the reason why he never wrote to thank us for our help. He was so very apologetic! I'm sure I haven't given a single thought to the question since he left us. But it was kind of him. He offered to pay some of my doctor's fees, too— seemed anxious to do something. Of course, I refused. In any case, he was sorry to miss you..."

Her mother's letter ran on to other subjects, and Bess scanned through the paragraphs, waiting in vain for the moment when she would return to the question of Tom Steele. Bess needed to know more. What had he said, precisely? In what way was he now "changed" or "distinguished"?

As she folded up the last sheet of her mother's letter, she decided that she would have to write to get more details, but it would be another week, at least, before her letter of inquiry had reached her mother and before her mother's own letter of response had come back. Suddenly the delay seemed unbearable to Bess.

The creak of the schoolroom door made Bess look up from her desk, just as her unruly pupil was slipping back into her chair. She saw the girl shake her head in response to the expectant looks of her friends, and heard her, quite distinctly, say, "It wasn't him."

"Miss Rose!" Bess exclaimed, feigning shock, and the girl looked at her guiltily. "I don't recall giving you permission to leave the schoolroom."

"You didn't, Miss Lanyard."

"Then what is your explanation?"

"I wanted to go downstairs for some fresh air. I will ask next time, miss."

"'Next time?'" Bess repeated, raising her eyebrows. Her mood of brief indulgence had evaporated, for reasons she did not care to examine—though they might have had something to do with what she had just read in her mother's letter. "I'm sure there won't *be* a next time, for as I'm sure you girls all know by now, the other teachers and I have agreed that you are to be confined to the school until all this silliness is over."

The girls all groaned. "It's no use grumbling now," Bess went on, with renewed fervour, "when you have all brought this punishment on yourselves by your giddy behaviour. Filling your heads with young men instead of attending to your studies… tell me, is developing your own vanity more important than developing your mind?"

AN OLD FACE

In the mutinous silence that followed, Bess looked around with satisfaction, and then started at the sound of a knock on the door. Without waiting for her response, Miss Kennedy, the principal, opened the door and fixed Bess with a stern look. For a moment, Bess thought she was going to be chided for letting one of her pupils out of her sight, but Miss Kennedy was apparently unaware of Rose Hamilton's little escapade, for she stayed only long enough to tell Bess that there was an officer waiting downstairs who was most anxious to speak to her.

Bess's heart leapt, with the initial, thrilling conclusion that it must be Mr Steele, but in the next moment, she voluntarily dashed her own hopes. Had she not just been lecturing her own girls about vanity and silliness? And what could be more vain or silly than thinking that Tom Steele, like the hero of a romance, would come to seek her out in Leeds? This officer seeking her out must be some misunderstanding.

Having reached this practical and cool decision, Bess got to her feet, ignoring the titters of her girls, and went downstairs, determined to straighten the matter out.

The edict of Miss Kennedy, that none of the girls in the school were to be allowed out, appeared also to extend to allowing any man in uniform over the threshold. Rather than finding him in the sitting-room, where any guests of the teachers were usually directed, Bess was obliged to go to the front door and step out into the street before she was greeted with her mysterious visitor.

Then, her heart leapt for a second time.

It was, indeed, Tom Steele.

When she looked past the gold epaulettes and red coat, she could still recognise him. Though his blond, shoulder-length locks had been shorn and a moustache and beard now covered what had once been all smooth chin, though his hand, as he grasped hers in enthusiastic greeting, was calloused where it had once been soft, the blue eyes that gazed out of his tanned face were unmistakable. In five years, she had never forgotten their exact shade: the colour of the sky on a cold, sunny winter's day.

As she peered at Tom, noticing all that had changed and all that had not, *he* peered at *her*, too, and when their hands had dropped to their sides again, he was the first to speak.

"Is this you, Bess?" he exclaimed. "But it *must* be you: I remember those very serious eyes of yours, very dark, too. Still…" Looking her over, "Well, you're quite grown up! A schoolmistress now, I hear! That's better than a governess, at least."

This was too much for Bess at once; he was too jesting, too familiar, speaking to her as though they were back in the parsonage at Ashford. "Yes, Mr Steele," she replied, and watched the change that came over his countenance on hearing her tones of cool politeness. "I work here."

"I suppose—you must be very surprised to see me," said Tom, after a moment's awkward silence. "I've just been to see your mother at Ashford."

"She told me in a letter," Bess said, inclining her head. "But I am still… very surprised, yes."

"You oughtn't to be. That is—well, of course I had to see you when I heard you were here!" Having made this declaration, Tom looked as though he didn't know what else to say, and he rubbed the back of his neck with one hand as his gaze strayed upwards. Then, abruptly, he said, "Someone's watching us."

Bess turned to follow his gaze and saw the faces of her pupils pressed up to the windows of the schoolroom. They didn't disperse when she met their gazes but smiled insolently down at her. "That is my class," she told Tom. "And I'd better go back up to them."

"Are they going to tease you, now that they've seen you with me?" said Tom, sympathetically, drawing his gaze back from the window to Bess. "I'm sorry. I didn't think…"

"You have nothing to apologise for, Mr Steele," Bess told him. "It was very kind of you to call on me."

"I should like to call on you again," he said, "so we can talk properly."

Bess ignored the swooping sensation in her stomach at his words and said, "Maybe some time, in Ashford…"

"Why not here?"

She looked at him uncertainly. "How long will you be in Leeds?"

"When do you get your next time off?" he countered.

Bess deliberated for a moment. "Saturday afternoon. But…"

"Saturday afternoon it is. Would you prefer if I called on you here or elsewhere?" Tom paused, seeing that she was about to make some protest. "What is it, what's wrong?"

"I hope," Bess said, keeping her tone as steady as she could, "that you will not delay your departure from Leeds on my account."

Tom made no response to this, just fixed his helmet back on and saluted her. His smile as they parted ways was still too familiar; it offended Bess's dignity, and she told herself that she didn't like it, though of course, as she found herself taking the stairs two steps at a time, and pausing outside the schoolroom door to observe that there was a warm, fizzy feeling inside her, which seemed to have spread right to her trembling fingertips, she was forced to admit that she *had* liked it; she had liked it very much.

A NOTE

The next two days dragged more than they had any right to do. As well as spending every waking moment trying to quell her own bursts of silliness—which mainly manifested in thoughts about Tom Steele, what he might be doing at that moment and whether *he* might be thinking about *her* too—Bess had to contend with the teasing of her pupils and the curiosity of her fellow staff.

The latter was especially vexing as the other teachers had never taken even a friendly interest in her before, yet now she was expected to answer any number of questions about the dashing young officer who had come to call for her. She downplayed her and Tom's acquaintance as best as she could, leaving out all the strange details of their first meeting while not outright lying, and, of course, made no mention of the fact that they had made some loose arrangement to meet on Saturday afternoon.

When a note arrived for her on Friday evening, it was thankfully at the time when everyone else was at dinner. Bess had been delayed a few minutes by the necessity of changing her dress, as an inkpot had been spilled on it earlier, and she was just descending the stairs to the dining room when one of the maids came in through the hall with a note.

Bess was able to intercept her, read the note and scribble a quick response without being observed by anyone else in the school, and when she took her seat at the teachers' table, she did so with such calm that she was sure none of them could have guessed at the riot of emotions within her.

Tom still wanted to meet tomorrow, and out of consideration for her, had suggested that they meet elsewhere, in a city park not far from the school. Bess had never seen his handwriting before; he wrote beautifully, and in the privacy of her own room that evening, she took out the note again just to trace the elaborate curl of each letter.

THE MEETING

I t was raining when she set out from the school the following afternoon. Bess had watched the skies all morning and traced with dismay the advance of grey clouds over Leeds. She had only a shawl over her head, but by keeping under shop awnings for the most part and ducking into doorways whenever the downpour got too heavy, she managed to avoid getting absolutely soaked.

When she got to the gates of the park, one glance told her that it was deserted, and she was on the point of turning back there and then, having no desire to get her shoes muddy. A hand touched her elbow, and Bess whirled around to see a gentleman with an umbrella beside her, whom she had passed moments before. "Oh," she said, foolishly.

"You just walked right past me," said Tom, with a laugh.

"Yes, I'm sorry, I was expecting you to be in your uniform." Bess squinted through the rain at him. He was wearing a dark green overcoat with a plaid cape over the shoulders, and together with his top hat and moustache, looked quite distinguished; she began to see what her mother had meant in her letter.

Tom lifted his umbrella until it was over both of their heads, and then said, "Don't you want to move in a bit closer? You're still getting wet."

"No, thank you, I'm perfectly fine," said Bess.

Tom gave her a sceptical look and then nodded to the street. "Well, why don't we get out of this? Find a tearoom somewhere to sit down."

"I shouldn't," said Bess. "People might see us, and talk. I'd prefer to walk instead: I really don't mind the rain."

"Maybe you don't, but I *do*." Tom looked around, frowning, and pointed to a gazebo in the park, whose roof was just visible through the trees. "Let's make for there, then."

This proposal was a bit more acceptable to Bess, and, relieved that he had not pressed the point, she followed him into the empty park. They fell into step with one another on the main path, and though Tom did not take her arm, Bess found herself drawing in, little by little, until she was fully under his umbrella.

"I was going to correct you last time," Tom said, "when you called me 'Mr.' You see, they made me a lieutenant in the army." Before Bess could say anything, he went on, "But since, as of yesterday, I have been officially discharged, it's perfectly all right for you to go on calling me 'Mr Steele.'"

"You were discharged here?" Bess exclaimed, staring at him.

"No, I got my orders the other day and went down to St John's barracks in London to present myself there."

"You went down to London and came back up here again?"

"Yes, why not?" Tom shrugged. "So now that we have peace again, I am a civilian once more. It's just as well, really, as a military career would be rather hard to reconcile with the duties of an Earl." Tom glanced at Bess for her reaction. "I inherited Branledge last year, after my father died."

"Oh! I am very sorry."

"I would like to say that I am too, but I'm not. I barely knew the man who died, even though he was my father." A fleeting sadness cross his otherwise bright eyes as he said it.

"You shouldn't say that," Bess told him, just as they came under the shelter of the gazebo.

"Whew!" Tom put down his umbrella, shaking off some of the excess drops, and leaned it against a pillar. "That's much better." He detached the plaid cape from the lapels of his overcoat and then fixed it around Bess's shoulders. "No arguing, now."

"You said just now that it is all right to call you 'Mr Steele,'" Bess said, "but if you're an Earl now…"

"Please don't call me 'Lord Steele.' If you do, I'll just laugh. It sounds positively ridiculous." Tom cast his gaze out at the deserted park and then looked back at Bess. "So, yes, the Earl is dead. I was in Crimea when I heard the news. My uncle has been keeping the estate for me since then. I owe it all to him, really."

"Your uncle?"

"Yes, you see, my father would have disinherited me, after what happened. I mean my 'incident.' Falling off my horse, staying with you and your mother, disappearing for days."

Bess was looking down at the ground now. She sensed Tom pausing, waiting to give her a chance to speak before he went on, "I suppose you thought I must have forgotten you, or that I didn't mean it when I promised to write."

"I can't remember what I thought," Bess lied. "It was so long ago."

"Of course. *I* remember very well, though. I wanted to do something for you—and not just to thank you and your mother, either. When you told me about how you were going to be a governess, I didn't like the idea of that: of you fending for yourself. I knew…" He hesitated. "… how good you are, and I thought people were sure to take advantage of that."

"People have been very kind to me," said Bess. That was another lie, of course; she felt alarmed by her sudden capacity for falsehood, which seemed to have sprung into being in the last five minutes.

"That may be so, but all the same, I wanted to do something for you. I *still* want to do something for you." Tom fixed his blue eyes on Bess with such intentness that she felt a little dizzy. "But, more than anything, I want you to know that I meant everything I said back then. It's just that when I got back to Branledge after leaving you…"

"I imagine you were in a bit of trouble."

"It was worse than I could have imagined." Tom walked around to the far end of the gazebo and then stopped, leaning one hand on the balustrade. Soon the skin there was flecked with raindrops, but he didn't seem to notice. "Like I said, my father would have disinherited me if not for my uncle. He would have done worse, in fact; he would have had locked me up in the house until I promised not to drink another drop of alcohol in my life. Of course, at that time I was never going to do that, to promise that, I mean. Not to the Earl. I would have gone on drinking myself into an early grave, just to spite him— what, are you cold?" Bess had given a shiver at his words.

She shook her head, and he continued, after eyeing her for a moment, "Uncle Reg knew that. So, he suggested a military career to my father. Offered to pay for my commission and everything. He said it would teach me discipline and restraint, so that when I came into my inheritance, I'd be able to shoulder the responsibility. He was wrong, of course; during my first year as an officer, I drank more than I ever drank at Oxford or at home."

Bess shook her head. In her mind's eye, she saw Mr Foster, swaying back and forth as he clutched a glass in his hand, his watery eyes fixed on her with predatory intent. She had not seen that picture so clearly in a long time. Suddenly, she was glad that there was a bit of distance between her and Tom.

"It's difficult to get away from the stuff," Tom was saying. "Really it is. And I was away from home, too, for the first time in my life, surrounded by strangers. Sometimes it was the only thing to do. You have to understand…" He stopped. "But you don't, do you?"

Bess met his gaze and said nothing. Tom's eyes searched her face for a moment before he continued, "You looked almost scared of me, just then. I've seen that look before—not on your face, though. You never seemed scared of me back then, when I was staying with you."

Bess wanted to speak, to tell him that it was not really him she was scared of. But then the picture of Mr Foster surged forward in her mind again, pouncing upon her again just when she thought that it had moved away. She broke Tom's gaze and looked down, blinking.

"Yes, I've seen that look before," Tom went on. "On my mother's face, after one of my very bad nights. That was long before I met you. You see, I was lost even back then, and she knew it. My father knew it, too. But he would have hated me even if I'd been a temperate saint like my brother. He could always find a reason, the Earl. There was always something wrong. Despite my earnest efforts, he treated me like a stranger, until..." Tom bowed his head, "until I simply gave up trying."

The plaid cape was beginning to slip off Bess's shoulders. She straightened it, and realised, as she did so, that every muscle in her body had tensed up as though preparing her for flight. Sensing Tom's eyes on her, she at last found her voice. "Are you still... lost?"

Tom shook his head. "No, I couldn't go on like that. It was bound to come to a crisis, some time or another. I thought it would happen when the war started, but I went on drinking even after that, even when we joined the fighting. I thought I was being careful. Keeping my senses sharp during the day—letting go only at night. But then one night, I was supposed to be keeping guard. The enemy sneaked into our camp and surprised us. I'd taken something to drink and fallen asleep. I woke up just in time to warn my comrades. But the thought of that—of the near miss, not just that I'd nearly got myself killed but everyone else too... that started to set me right. There were other things that set me right, too. That look on my mother's face." Tom was silent for a moment. "And maybe meeting you and Mrs Lanyard, who were so good and kind to me when I didn't deserve it."

"You *did* deserve it," Bess insisted, before she could help herself, and Tom met her gaze, smiling. He pushed off the balustrade and took a step towards her.

"That sounds more like the old Bess. I mean—Miss Lanyard."

"You can call me Bess," she said, feeling herself blushing.

"Are you sure?" He stopped a few feet from her. As she nodded, he said, "Then you must call me Tom."

"I can't do *that*." She gave a quick shake of the head.

"Well, whatever you do, don't call me Lord Steele, all right? That's all I ask."

Bess smiled and nodded. Tom picked up his top hat from where he had placed it on the balustrade, fiddled with it for a moment and then put it down again. "I want you to understand," he said, turning towards her. "I don't do any of that anymore."

"So, you became a 'temperate saint?'" she said, pointedly.

"Like my brother?" Tom laughed, darkly. "Not the saint part, at least not a first perhaps, but the temperance part… well, that was quite necessary. And when I stopped, I found myself thinking more clearly than ever before. For the last two years, fighting in Crimea I was reminded every awful day how fleeting this life is. I remembered your prayers, and your devotion to something bigger than yourself. Despite all of my rebellion, and the terrible things I have said and done, the words of Scripture became more real to me than the nose on my face..."

Bess leaned in, eager to hear.

"The only way I can describe it is that something broke through to my heart. God touched my heart and changed the way I see everything. All I could think about from that day was living long enough so that I could get back to England. So that I could meet you again and show you that it wasn't all empty words, that I never did forget...."

Bess's heart had been twisting painfully as he spoke, finding Tom's confession shining a light on her own secret thoughts, but now she forced herself to interrupt. "Mr Steele, you have no obligation to us. I *am* glad you've sought us out again, and I'm sure my mother is, too. But we don't expect any thanks for what we did. We would have done the same for any man."

Tom stared at her for a moment, and then nodded to himself. "I'm sure you would have."

"And, really..." Bess continued, though every word she uttered seemed to sink her own heart, "it was not necessary for you to go to so much trouble to come to Leeds and find me, when you have so many other things to do. I'm glad, of course, but I don't expect—"

"I know you don't. And will it put your mind at ease to hear that I didn't just come here for you? You remember my friend Harry, the one I was staying with when I got lost and found myself at your house? He lives here now, has made a killing in speculation. I have been catching up with him while I'm here—so you see, it hasn't all been sacrifice on my part." He was grinning at her, and, like before, his grin was impossibly infectious. Bess smiled back, feeling the last remnants of tension leaking out of her body.

"And I intend to spend some more time here catching up with dear Harry," Tom went on, grandly, "before I assume my position as lord and heir of Branledge Hall. So, if you'll allow me, I'd like to see you again, Bess."

"You don't have to—"

"I *know* I don't have to, but I would like to." Tom gestured out to the park. "Look at that, the rain stopped, and I didn't even notice, because I was so busy talking about myself." He raised his eyebrows. "The next time—if you're willing—I should like to hear all about you, and what you've been doing these last few years, and the people you've met, and the places you've been to…"

"If you're intent on being bored to tears," Bess said, "then I suppose I can't stop you."

Tom laughed. "Yes, I am intent, Miss Lanyard. And now I'd better get you back to your school, while this rain holds off."

PURE HAPPINESS

Bess had always wondered, as anyone who has known hardship and sorrow early in life might wonder, whether there was such a thing as pure happiness. People like Laura Foster, she thought, who threw caution to the wind and plunged headfirst into the pursuit of their own desires, might experience something like pure happiness upon the gratification of those desires. But such happiness could not be long-lasting, as a new desire would soon replace the old, and so Bess had never really sought it out for herself.

She discovered, however, during the next fortnight that Tom Steele stayed in Leeds, that knowing that one's happiness was bound to come to an end sooner or later did not in any way diminish or tarnish it. They saw one another every few days, either in the evenings when Bess got off work, or during her free afternoons. Saturdays were the days when they could spend the most time together, as Sundays tended to be full with bringing the girls to church or—now, following Miss Kennedy's edict forbidding them from going out—reading the Bible to them in the schoolroom, and one of the teachers generally had to be on hand to cook the evening meal, since that was the servants' day off.

So, a happier two weeks swept in to replace those two weeks that still stood out in Bess's memory, from five years ago. To discover that she had not been forgotten was one thing. To discover that she could still talk to Tom as a friend and equal, even though he was twenty-six and she was eighteen, even though he was rich and she was poor, even though he had travelled the world and she had never even been to London, was quite another. They had both been through enough changes to turn them into complete strangers to one another. It seemed a miracle to Bess, therefore, that they were still able to understand each other just as they had done before.

But that was not the only wondrous thing about those two weeks. Leeds, the smoky, bristly city, became like a fairyland to Bess. Every street that she and Tom discovered together seemed to hold its own special charm.

When it rained, they would huddle together under Tom's umbrella. When the sun shone, they would walk through the parks, where cherry-blossom petals dotted the pathways and grass, as though they had been scattered there for the honour of being trodden on by Tom and Bess.

One Saturday, Tom took Bess out to the countryside to visit the ruins of an old castle, along with his friend Harry and Harry's sister, both of whom were so kind to Bess for that whole day that she felt as though she had strayed into some other world. On another occasion, he persuaded her to visit a teashop, far enough away from the school that they would not be observed by anyone they knew, and they sat there for hours without running out of things to talk about.

But the times when they were alone, unobserved, and walking through Leeds, were the best times for Bess. When they were side by side, she was able to be more honest with Tom than if they had been facing one another across a table.

She told him, hands shaking, of the circumstances around her dismissal from Ashford Hall, and he took her arm in his and pressed it close to his side and did not let go of it for a long time. He told her of other things that had been lost to him due to his drinking—his brother's trust, which had been worn down after countless loans that Tom had not paid him back, and his engagement to the girl that his parents had chosen for him, a girl who had broken things off after Tom had missed one of their appointments to go to the races with his friends. All of this had been before he had met Bess, as he was quick to assure her, and the fact that he connected those two events in his mind—his engagement to the girl and his meeting Bess—made her smile afterwards, though she kept that secret smile to herself.

Neither of them had spoken of any feelings beyond friendship. Bess knew what she was feeling, and the last thing she wanted was to spoil that happy time by finding out, once and for all, that Tom did not share it.

ILL TIDINGS

At school, Bess sailed through her lessons in a way she never had before, and comments from pupils and teachers alike seemed to roll right off her shoulders. She felt herself to be emanating a sort of general benevolence. But when, one day, a letter arrived for her, addressed in what was unmistakably Laura Foster's handwriting, she tucked the envelope away in her drawer and took a couple of days to decide what to do with it. She even thought of throwing it away, concluding that whatever Laura was writing to her about, it couldn't be anything good. It wasn't until one afternoon, an hour before she was to go meet Tom in town, that Bess found her conscience stirred. She went to the drawer, opened the envelope in a rush, and staggered back as she read the first few lines.

"Dear Miss Lanyard," Laura had written. "I know that I must be the last person you want to hear from. But please don't throw away this letter until you have read what I have to say. I have been entrusted with a secret which I think you deserve to know. Your mother is dying. I have been in to see her every day for the past week, and the surgeon has told me that there is not long left. But she won't admit it and says you're not to be sent for or bothered. I don't know why she should be so stubborn, when of course you would want to be kept in the loop about these things, but..."

Bess dropped the letter without reading the rest, and sat down, hard, on the edge of her bed. She put her hands on either side of her head and stared at the shaft of sunlight on the opposite wall, watching as every now and then the shadow of the curtain, stirred by a breeze, split it in half.

She had not written her usual weekly letter to her mother. The last one that she had sent had been last week, and in it, she had told her all about how Tom had come straight from Ashford to Leeds to meet her, how they were meeting pretty often, and how happy she was in his company. Just as they had made no mention of love to one another, she had made no mention of it in the letter to her mother, but she thought it had been pretty well understood all the same. And now it seemed that it *had* been understood, all too well, for her mother, rather than sending for her now, preferred her to stay and be happy.

Bess rose from her bed in a flash and crossed the room, picking up the letter from where it had fallen on the floor. Reading the date on the top, she saw that it had been sent almost a week ago. And then she had taken two days to open it… she felt sick with guilt.

She just about held back her tears as she went downstairs to tell Miss Kennedy about what had happened; they burst out as soon as she was back in her room, and she threw herself back on her bed and stared up at the ceiling. It was too late to get a train; she would have to wait till the following morning, by which time it might be too late; it might be too late *now*.

Bess had never felt so useless in all her life. She lay there as the shaft of sunlight crept across the wall and disappeared, and as the light in the room greyed out. She heard the bell ring to summon all the staff and pupils to their meals but did not go down. She heard their feet trooping up the stairs afterwards, their loud voices offending her ears.

TOO LATE

It was fully dark when she heard a knock on her door, and the maid came in to tell her that she had a visitor downstairs. Bess only realised at that moment that she had missed her appointment with Tom. She got up, pushed her feet into the boots that lay at the end of her bed, and tied back her hair loosely behind her head, for it had fallen in messy strands around her face over the past few hours. She trooped down the stairs and found the maid waiting for her in the hall.

"He's in the sitting-room, miss," the maid told her, and Bess, even in her current state, was struck by the grandeur of this concession; she had been expecting to have to meet her guest at the door, just as she had had to do the first time he had called here.

Tom sprang up out of his chair as Bess entered, and came forward, taking her hands in his own. "I heard about your mother. That woman told me, your principal—she turned me away when I called earlier today, but when I called again a few minutes ago, she told me to come in and wait. She said you hadn't come down for dinner, and that someone ought to speak to you."

"I'm sorry about earlier," Bess told him. "I didn't think—I wasn't—"

"Of course, you didn't. Come here, sit down." He led her to the seat he had just vacated, got her to sit, and then sat himself on the edge of the nearest chair, leaning towards her.

"How did she look, when you saw her?" Bess was afraid to meet his gaze when she asked the question. "When you were in Ashford, a few weeks ago?"

Tom hesitated a moment before replying. "She looked weak… perhaps. Thinner and more tired than I remember her looking back when I first stayed with you."

"She is. The last few years have not been easy on her. And ever since my father died, she's never really…" Bess turned towards him suddenly, unable to hide the desperation in her voice. "But I thought we'd have longer. I knew she wasn't well, but I didn't think this would come so suddenly."

As the tears blurred her eyes, clotted her dark eyelashes and then started to fall again, she heard Tom sigh, almost imperceptibly, and then get out of his seat. He came to stand beside her chair, and paused, making a motion for one of her hands, but one was covering her cheek and the other was clenched tight on the back of her chair. Tom put a hand to her shoulder instead. His voice, when he spoke, had an earnestness to it that she was unaccustomed to hearing. "I suppose you want to go right away."

"I *can't*," Bess moaned. "The first train doesn't leave till tomorrow morning, at seven. And anything might have happened by then…"

"You don't have to travel by train. You can go by post instead."

"Post is expensive."

"You don't have to worry about that."

Bess turned to look up at Tom. His hand shifted from her shoulder to the spot just below her neck, resting very lightly there.

"No arguments," he said. "You saved my life, Bess. I think I can afford to pay for one seat in a post-chaise."

JOURNEY

As it turned out, Tom ended up paying for two seats, since he insisted on going with Bess, and despite the late hour, despite the fact that one of the manservants at the school had been perfectly willing to act as her escort instead, he would not be persuaded otherwise. At first, he agreed that he would only accompany her as far as Bradford. But it seemed that had been only to placate her, for when they had reached the coach inn at the outskirts of town, Tom went inside with her to wait while the horses were being changed and showed no signs of leaving.

Bess, who seemed to be experiencing a dozen emotions a minute—fear and worry and sorrow all mixing with that old happiness in Tom's company—felt quite annoyed at this and reminded her companion of their compromise. They were sitting in the dark taproom, which was utterly empty, their only source of light being a lantern that the porter had loaned them when they had come in.

In the pool of orange light, Tom's eyes shone a strange shade, and his expression was hard to read as he shook his head on hearing Bess's protest. "Of course, I'm going with you the whole way."

"But we agreed…"

"I'm not going to let you travel alone at this time of night, Bess."

"But it's nearly morning," she said weakly. Tom sighed, resting his elbows on the table and averting his gaze as if he, too, were now annoyed.

"Close your eyes for a bit," he said. "The porter will come in and tell us when the horses have been changed. I'll watch out for him."

Bess looked at him doubtfully. But the invitation was too tempting to pass up; her eyelids, which had been growing heavier and heavier the longer they sat in that warm, dim room, now began to drift closed. It seemed only a minute or two later that Tom was gently shaking her shoulder, telling her it was time to go. She got up, groggy and clumsy, and was faintly aware of his arm around her shoulders as they went out through the yard, taking their seats in the carriage.

For the remaining part of the journey, Bess slept. As light began to creep into the carriage, she drifted in and out of wakefulness. Every time she woke, she expected Tom to be gone, but he would always be there, sitting across from her. On one occasion, opening her eyes to find him watching her, Bess adjusted the blanket that had been draped over her and mumbled, "You should... go back to Branledge."

"I will, soon," Tom told her, quietly. "Now go back to sleep."

BE NOT AFRAID

Bess found the vicar's wife, Mrs Poole, in the cottage at Ashford when she arrived. It was comforting to find that her mother had not been left alone, and it struck Bess for the first time that it was a good thing they had been obliged to leave the parsonage, even if it still wrenched her heart to think of someone else living in their home, climbing *her* hill. If they had still been living in that remote place, she knew that not as many friends and neighbours would have been on hand to help her mother—not as many as, judging by what Mrs Poole told her, had come to see Mrs Lanyard during the past week alone.

Their number included, of course, Mr Newman, and Miss Foster, and well as Miss Collins, and some other names which Bess had not heard since her childhood—names which she had hoped never to hear again. That these people had called on her mother, and had wanted to be remembered kindly to Bess, filled her with such strange emotion that she resolved not to think about it; she had enough emotions to contend with at that moment.

Once she saw that Bess was settled, Mrs Poole took her leave to go back to the parsonage. Bess, seating herself by her mother's bedside, placed a hand over the one that lay above the covers. She listened for a moment to her mother's soft, slow breathing, and wondered if, after all, there had been some mistake. Perhaps Miss Foster had been exaggerating in her letter—as she had been known to do in the past. Mrs Poole, after all, had not said a single word about anyone dying to Bess, and had seemed to think that a little rest and care would restore Mrs Lanyard to her former self. But just as Bess was beginning to follow this train of thought, her mother's eyes fluttered open, and she looked at her as though she could not believe what she saw.

"Bess." Her voice was very low. "You're here."

"Yes, Mother." Bess had determined not to cry, not yet, and she felt herself waver in her conviction for only a moment. "And I'll stay with you until you're feeling better."

Mrs Lanyard squeezed Bess's hand, with the lightest of pressures. "What about the school?" she asked. "What about… Mr Steele?"

"It's all been taken care of, Mother." Bess returned the pressure, rubbing her thumb over the back of her mother's hand, which was rough and careworn. "Mr Steele wished to be remembered to you. He brought me here, you see, from Leeds, and he must get back to his estate in Somerset so he couldn't stay."

"That is... very kind," murmured her mother.

"Yes, he has been a great friend to me, these last few weeks."

"Friend?" Mrs Lanyard repeated, and though it was difficult to tell with her drowsiness, the expression that she was giving Bess now seemed to be sceptical. Bess thought of her parting from Tom a little while ago, of how he had at last agreed to leave her, and of the overwhelming relief that she had felt once he had kissed her hand and walked back to the carriage—once he had been borne away out of her sight. He hadn't seemed to fit with the scene; he had seemed too big for a small street in Ashford, somehow. It was right for him to go back to Branledge. It was right for Bess and Mrs Lanyard to remember him fondly this time, even if he did, once more, disappear from their lives without a trace.

"Yes, Mother," she said, nodding. "A friend."

Mrs Lanyard turned her head sideways on the pillow, as though to get a better look at her daughter. "I know about Mr Newman," she told her, and Bess stared. "That you turned him down. He told me, one of the times that he came to visit here."

"Were you—are you… angry?" Bess asked, and her mother just smiled.

"No, dear, I'm not angry. I suppose he was the one who sent for you?"

"No, it was Miss Foster who wrote to me." Bess registered the faint surprise in her mother's eyes before she went on, unable to help herself, "But why didn't you send for me yourself? I can't bear thinking of you like this, with no one—"

"I have not been lonely, Bess."

"Maybe not, but you should have written…"

"I would have sent for you, at the last," Mrs Lanyard said, and Bess felt herself freeze. "I just wanted to give you… a little more time, before you had to come back."

It might have been difficult, before, to read the expression in her mother's eyes, but there was no mistaking the certainty there now. "Before you start arguing, Bess," her mother said, watching her. "Listen to what I have to say. I'm not afraid. Remember your father, even when he was suffering so greatly, even at the very end—how he never complained, how he always told us that it was God's will? I could not be married to such a man for twenty-five years without finding some of that same courage myself."

Bess could not stop the tears now. "Darling girl," her mother said again—she had never used such words with Bess before. "I'm not afraid."

"But *I* am," Bess choked out, and she brought her mother's hand up to her cheek, clutching it in both of hers as she shook with sobs.

"Then let's pray," said Mrs Lanyard, gently. "So that God might grant *you* courage, too."

A CHANGED LIFE

The shadows stretched long across the walls of her mother's room, and the lace curtain over the window fluttered in the evening breeze. Bess had been sitting by her mother's bedside all day, and was nearly asleep when she heard the knock on the front door of the cottage. She got up and walked out of the room, like one in a dream, to greet her guest.

Laura Foster, just as beautiful as Bess remembered, stood on the doorstep, with Mr Newman by her side. They both started to see her, and Laura was the first to speak.

"So, it's true: you're here at last! I was so afraid that you might have thrown away my letter—I wouldn't have blamed you if you did. Oh, Miss Lanyard..." She surged forward to give Bess an impulsive embrace—the first such gesture that she had ever made in all the time that they had known each other. Bess met it coldly, stiffly, and she saw the change in Laura's expression as she drew back again: the way her fair eyebrows drew down in a frown, and the way she bit her lip.

Mr Newman was next, and he shook Bess's hand, murmuring his greeting in his own restrained, earnest way.

They sat with her for a while in the drawing room, talking a little of the news of Ashford. At one point, Laura began to describe her London season, making sure to emphasise how dull it had been—but then, evidently seeing that Bess had no interest in hearing about it, and that Mr Newman was looking very grave, she broke off and murmured that she had been glad to come home again.

Mrs Lanyard was still sleeping, and every now and then during the visit, Bess would excuse herself to go and check on her. Each time she came back, Mr Newman and Laura would look around guiltily upon her entrance, as though they had been in silent conference with one another. Some of Bess's natural curiosity returned to her at this, and she wondered just how far their acquaintance had advanced in her absence. Perhaps there was already an understanding between them? If so, then Mr Newman had certainly been soon consoled after his disappointment at Bess's hands.

Alarmed and a little ashamed at this last bitter thought, Bess found herself incapable of joining the conversation, and sat in silence while Mr Newman talked to Laura about some tenants of her father's, one of whom was also ill. "I have no time to see them today," he said, "for there is another family, that lives a little further away, whom I must visit."

"Then *I* will go," said Laura at once. "Ought I to bring them something from the Hall?"

"It would be a great consolation to them, if you did," said Mr Newman quietly, "though I'm sure it is not expected."

Practically bursting with eagerness, Laura got up from her chair and gathered up her things. "Miss Lanyard," she said cautiously as she was tying her bonnet. "I hope I may call on you soon again."

"If you wish," said Bess blandly, and submitted to a kiss on her cheek from her former pupil without a change in her own countenance. As Laura hurried out, Bess felt Mr Newman's eyes on her.

"You see," he said, after a long pause, "that Miss Foster is quite changed."

"Is she?" said Bess pointedly. "Excuse me, I must check on my mother." She rose from her seat, and Mr Newman copied her movement, following her just to the door of her mother's bedroom. As Bess went to straighten the bedclothes, adjusting them so that they covered her mother more securely, Mr Newman stood in the threshold.

"Perhaps you might not see it yet, Miss Lanyard," he continued. "Since you have been away. But *I* have been here, and since Miss Foster returned from London a few weeks ago, I have seen that she is indeed changed. You know that the season is not finished yet, and will not be for another month or so? But she came away against her cousins' wishes and removed herself from that scene. And, well, you heard her speak of it: it is evident that the charms of such a place are not for her."

Bess said nothing, picking up the tray on her mother's bedside and carrying it out. Mr Newman stood aside to let her pass and followed her into the kitchen as she went to set it down there. "I know that she wrote to you, to summon you here," he said. "In fact, I advised her against it, thinking that we ought to honour Mrs Lanyard's wishes in this matter. But not long after Miss Foster had sent the letter to you, your mother took a turn for the worse. I think… on this occasion, that I was mistaken, and that Miss Foster was right to write to you when she did."

"Yes," said Bess, taking the dishes off her mother's tray one by one—first the bowl, then the cup, then the spoon. "I am certainly glad that she did."

"Then…" Mr Newman hesitated a moment before continuing, "well, then, I think you might show your gratitude a bit better."

"My *gratitude?*" Bess turned around to face him. Mr Newman looked at her steadily.

"Yes, Miss Lanyard. Your gratitude. I know that it must be as clear to you as it is to me, that Miss Foster would like to be your friend at this time—and that it would be the greatest kindness you could show, if you let her."

At a loss for words, Bess led the way out into the drawing room. "*I'm* not the one who…" she began, and then stopped, shaking her head.

"Perhaps you feel that, because she was not your friend before, she has no right to be now." Mr Newman paused, and then, seeming to take her silence as confirmation, went on, "But I can reassure you on that point. Miss Foster, being away at the time that her father dismissed you, knew nothing of the matter. It was not until she came back that she heard about what had happened, and then…"

"I was still in Ashford at that time," Bess said. "She might have called on me."

"She was weak, Miss Lanyard. She was ashamed. But if you could see how she regrets it now! If you could see that, you would not be talking as you are." Mr Newman sighed. "I don't know what quarrel came between you before—what caused Miss Foster to go to Manchester so suddenly as she did. But I know that she would like to have a second chance, to show herself to be your friend."

"Then she may talk to me herself," Bess said. "Rather than sending you as an intermediary."

"I am no intermediary, Miss Lanyard," said Mr Newman, with a small smile. "I have merely observed some things which I think ought to be set right. Miss Foster will talk to you of this matter herself, if you give her the chance. But you must lead by example in this. She was your pupil once, remember? She looks up to you…"

"She always said I could never teach her anything," Bess interrupted. "I don't believe she ever saw me as anything more than a servant."

"She looks up to you," Mr Newman repeated. "And whether you believe it or not, I know that you will do what is right. You always do." After he had uttered those last words, he looked down as if embarrassed, and Bess wondered if he was remembering his offer to her.

"I will try…" she said after a moment, and then stopped, uncertainly. But this seemed to be enough; Mr Newman looked up again, his countenance brightening, and came towards her to shake her hand.

"That is all I ask. Until tomorrow, Bess. Remember me to your mother, and may God watch over you both."

MOTHER

A little under a week later, Mrs Lanyard closed her eyes on the world, and followed her husband's voice, through the breeze that stirred the trees on the hill over their old house. That voice which had once called her to wake after a long sleep now called her to rest forever.

Bess was now an orphan, but she had never felt less alone in the world.

Friends and neighbours came from all quarters to help her with those arrangements that were too much for her. Mr Newman performed the service, and Laura stayed by Bess's side through it all, her arm joined with hers. Mr Foster, being in London, was absent, for which Bess could not be sorry, though he did send a letter of formal condolence. *That* was one letter which she did not hesitate to throw away.

Tom wrote from Somerset to inquire after her mother, and then wrote again once Bess had told him the news. He had warned her once, long ago, that he was a poor correspondent, and she began to see now what he had meant: though his handwriting was beautiful, and the tone of his letter warm and friendly, the style was distracted. He would start one subject before running headlong into another. As she read the words that he had written, Bess had a picture of him sitting in his office at Branledge, writing a line or two before being interrupted by the entry of his financial agent, or solicitor, or butler. The letter would lie there on the desk for an hour or two, perhaps, before he returned to it, without quite remembering where he had left off.

She wrote back once more to thank him, hoping, at the same time, to make it clear by her tone that she did not expect anything more from him, after such friendship as he had already shown.

But it seemed that everyone was surprising her these days, for Tom wrote back once more with a very kind invitation to Bess to come and stay at Branledge whenever she liked. Miss Kennedy from the school wrote, too, telling Bess that she could have until the end of the month to get her and her mother's affairs in order—which meant that she could not produce the excuse of work in response to Tom's invitation. There was no way she could accept it, she knew, but she could not think how best to refuse, and was still deliberating over the letter when another invitation came.

Laura, now alone at Ashford Hall, wanted very much for her former governess to join her there, this time as a friend and guest. Bess's first instinct was to refuse this, too, given her memories of that place, and the fact that, while she had tried her best to follow Mr Newman's advice, there was still an awkwardness between her and her former pupil which no number of friendly overtures could dispel. But as Mr Foster was still away in London, and as Bess's business in finding a new tenant for her and her mother's cottage might just as well be conducted from the Hall as from Ashford itself, she at last accepted. She was glad to leave that silent house, where her mother had breathed her last, even if the one into which she now entered held some of its own horrors for her.

By now, Bess could not deny that Mr Newman had been right; there *was* a change in Laura, and it became even more clear now that Bess was in close quarters with her. They had no lessons anymore, and yet Laura spent more of her time with Bess than she had ever had before, simply sitting, listening to her read aloud, or discussing with her some book or painting or piece of music that had struck her recently.

Their new domain was the drawing room, which did not have as good a fire as the schoolroom. But they did not need one, most of the time; that spring was mild, and even the squalls of wind and rain that lashed the windows of the Hall never lasted for long.

"I used to hate the weather here," Laura told Bess, after rushing to latch the window during one of those squalls. "But when I was in London, I found myself missing it. Isn't that strange?"

Bess did not think it was strange at all. All the reports that she had heard of London, from Mr Steele, her mother and her students at Leeds, described it as a foggy and dirty place. But, sensing something in Laura's tone that suggested a confession was imminent, she refrained from giving her own opinion, and said instead, "Still, I imagine the parties and balls took your mind off it. I have heard that you made quite an impression there."

"Oh, I suppose I did." With some of her former languor, Laura went back to her chair and slouched into it. "Some of those nights I hardly remember. I'd get so dizzy from the wine—"

"Laura!" Bess exclaimed, horrified.

"Why, everyone was drinking it, Miss Lanyard, and of course I would only have a glass or two. It wasn't just that, that turned my head: it was everything glittering so bright you can't imagine, and the women so dazzling, and the men so refined and graceful, and then the dancing—round and round in circles till I couldn't stand it anymore, and feeling all those eyes on me, and knowing that people thought things about me that they had no right to think, and had decided things about me without saying so much as a word to my face…"

"It sounds—rather overwhelming," Bess agreed.

"Do you know who I would find myself thinking about, whenever I got back to my cousins' house after one of those parties?"

Bess was grateful that Laura did not pause long enough for her to give her answer, for she would have said "Mr Newman," and was surprised to hear instead, from her friend's lips, "My mother."

"Your mother?" Bess repeated.

"Yes." Laura picked up the muslin shawl that she had been embroidering but showed little inclination to return to the work. She stared at the material as she said, "I would see all those other mothers at the balls, sitting away from the dancing and talking, talking, pointing out their daughters to each other. And I would think, when I got home, how unfair it was that my mother couldn't be there with me—how she'd been taken away just when I needed her most."

There was a long silence. "You have never talked about your mother with me before," Bess said, gently.

"I know." Laura looked up suddenly. "I suppose you thought I was going to say I was thinking about Mr Newman all the time, while I was in London. But, you know, the funny thing is, I hardly thought of him at all. It

179

wasn't just because I was meeting so many other young men. It was because I couldn't imagine him there, wedged into the corner in the card-room, or dancing a set with some young lady—with *me*. I couldn't imagine it." Laura gave a quick, sad kind of smile, and picked up her embroidery again. "I wanted to be able to picture him there, but I couldn't. That was when I knew that there was something wrong."

"Then," Bess prompted, after a moment, "you don't feel...?"

Laura did not meet her gaze as she said, "He's a friend, now. I missed you such a great deal when you were gone and felt so badly about how I'd left things with you. When I came back from London to this old place, with only Father for company, it was even worse. Mr Newman understood it all, without my having to explain. I couldn't tell him the reason for our quarrel, of course—" Here she stammered a bit before continuing, "But he knew I wanted to make things right."

Bess, at this point, felt it necessary to explain to Laura how Mr Newman had persuaded her to give her another chance. Laura listened in silence, still not meeting Bess's gaze, and when it was over, she said faintly, "Well, that was kind of him."

"I wonder if it was just kind," Bess said, remembering how Mr Newman's face had lit up when she had said that she would try to give Laura a second chance. "I wonder…" But Laura looked up and shook her head.

"Please, Miss Lanyard. Please don't say it. I've only just got out of all that foolish thinking about him. If I hear something that makes me hope—then I might fall right into it again."

"Very well," said Bess, after a moment. "I understand." As they went on sewing in silence, she looked across at her former pupil, and wondered if Laura knew how much Bess really meant those words.

PROMISES KEPT

I t was Bess who first heard the news. Laura was out at the time, visiting one of her father's tenants, and Bess was in her room at Ashford Hall, packing her things. She planned to leave for Leeds the next day, for it was now the end of May and as there was a whole month left before the summer holidays, the school could not do without her for much longer. She still had not managed to find someone to rent the cottage in her and her mother's place, but the landlord had written to tell her that he would manage the matter himself, and Bess was glad to have the responsibility taken out of her hands.

She was half-expecting a call from Mr Newman, for he had told her last Sunday after church that he would come to see her before her departure, and so she was not surprised when one of the maids came to her room to summon her downstairs. But when she met the butler in the hallway, and saw his grim face, she came to an abrupt halt. "What is it, Andrews?"

"We've had word from London, miss, about the master. One of my staff, who was attending him there, travelled back on purpose this morning to tell us…" The butler hesitated. "Well, perhaps we'd better wait until Miss Foster gets home before discussing it."

"Yes," said Bess, half-relieved, half-apprehensive. "Perhaps we'd better."

The next few hours seemed to crawl by, with no sign of Laura. Bess paced up and down the drawing room, and eventually came to a decision: she would find the butler, acquaint herself with what had happened, and go to find Laura and deliver the message herself. It was better than waiting here in suspense, and she was sure that her friend would not mind her taking such a liberty on this occasion.

She rushed downstairs again and met Mr Newman in the hall; he had just been shown in by the maid and was breathing hard as though he had been running. "You have heard the news?" he asked her, without preamble, and his eyes darted past her, searching the hall as though he expected to see someone else there apart from the maid. "Where is Miss Foster?"

Bess told him, and Mr Newman gave a start. "You mean, she doesn't know yet? But it's all over town—I heard it as I was coming through the post office." He stared at Bess, as though struck by a new and frightening idea. "Suppose

Miss Foster hears about it from one of the tenants, who thinks she must know already? What a way that would be to find out…"

"I thought so myself, and I was on the point of going to look for her," Bess explained, as patiently as she could, "except that I still don't know what I am to tell her, if I did. But you evidently do, Mr Newman. What has happened to Mr Foster?"

Mr Newman ran a hand through his brown hair, looking a little frantic. "He is dead," he told Bess. "I understand that he was at a party two nights ago—that he had a good deal to drink and then tried to make his way home on foot. He was found in the street yesterday, and this morning one of his servants travelled back from town to give the household the news. Except…" His gaze strayed past Bess. "Except, Miss Foster is not here!"

"Then let's go find her together," Bess suggested, gently. "Wait here for me, and I will go fetch my things."

But when she got back downstairs, having swapped her slippers for boots and taken a shawl from her room, it was to find the front door standing wide open, and Mr Newman gone. "He wouldn't stay, miss," the maid told her, and Bess nodded, deliberating a moment.

"Then I will follow him," she said at last, and set out into the grounds. As she walked, she thought again of the frantic look on Mr Newman's face. Of course, while not being able to feel sorry that such a man was dead, and therefore could do no more harm to anyone, Bess was still worried about how her friend would take the news. But her worry had not approached the level of Mr Newman's, and she wondered why.

She did not have to search far to find her two friends. As she was walking through the shrubbery, she heard the soft sound of someone crying, and the low tones of Mr Newman. Seeing through the leaves a flash of white muslin, Bess came to a stop and peered around the corner, to where the path curved around a bench before continuing on to the woods. Standing by the bench was Mr Newman, and Laura was in his arms. Her bonnet had fallen off, and her face was hidden from view, buried in his shoulder. She was shaking a little, and Mr Newman held her steady, one hand moving back and forth across her shoulder blades as he said words that Bess could not hear. Looking at the expression on his face, Bess had her answer to the question that had just been plaguing her mind.

A SECOND PROPOSAL

Bess wanted to delay her departure by a day, in order to see that her friend was all right, but both Mr Newman and Laura insisted that she should keep to her commitment and go. The former accompanied Bess in the Fosters' carriage as far as Bradford, while Laura stayed behind to see to her father's funeral arrangements.

They both sat silent for the first part of the journey, but Bess could see that her companion had something on his mind. It was evident from the way that Mr Newman kept shifting back and forth in his seat, casting a glance out the window every few minutes, and then sighing as though disappointed by what he saw.

"Bess—I mean, Miss Lanyard," he said at length.

Bess told him that, at this point in their friendship, it was perfectly all right to call her "Bess," and then met his look of appeal with a patient smile. "What is it?"

"I would like to ask your opinion on something. That is…" Mr Newman rubbed his chin with his hand, and his gaze flickered away from Bess. "… something happened between me and Miss Foster, yesterday, after I went to tell her the news about her father."

"I know," said Bess, and his eyes grew very wide. "I went looking for you and saw you together."

"Then—you saw…"

"I saw you embracing."

"That wasn't all." Mr Newman screened his eyes with his hand as he spoke his next words to Bess. "I don't know what came over me but seeing her like that—so shocked and distressed—I'm afraid I got a bit carried away. I started to promise her all kinds of things."

"What things, exactly?" Bess said, a little sternly.

Mr Newman swallowed. "Well… I might have told her that she would never have to be alone again. And I might have said that, if she allowed me to, I would like to take care of her for the rest of our lives."

There was a silence, broken only by another of Mr Newman's sighs. Bess said then, "And did she say that she would? Allow you to take care of her?"

"She did not say in—so many words, but I think it was pretty well understood." Mr Newman lowered his hand

and looked directly at Bess again, fearfully. "The trouble is, I have already accepted a post in Hampshire."

"Hampshire?" Bess repeated, staring at him.

"Yes, I was never going to stay in Ashford for good, you know. I was only supposed to be there for six months. But meeting such friends as you and your mother, and…"

"And Miss Foster," Bess prompted.

Mr Newman reddened. "And, yes, Miss Foster… I was talked into staying a little longer by Mr Poole. But this new post in Hampshire would be much more suitable for me, really. I would be closer to my brother and his wife, closer to the town where I grew up. I would be working in a larger parish, so there would be more for me to do. I could do a lot more good than I do here." He paused. "I have told no one about this yet, Bess."

"Then you may count on my silence."

"Thank you. You are… everything that is good." Mr Newman's expression turned from fearful to considering as he looked at her. "Long ago, Bess, when I asked you a question, your answer was no. I wonder if your answer would still be the same, if I were to ask it again today?"

"Mr Newman…"

"I remember you said, then, that you did not think you liked me well enough to marry me, and that you feared my own feelings might be similarly… limited. But there is no one whose company I enjoy more. And now that you are alone—please don't interrupt just yet, Bess—now that you are alone, I should like to offer my hand to you. Before your dear mother passed, I promised her that I would take care of you."

Bess was so flabbergasted that it took her a minute to realise that he had paused to let her speak, and another minute before she could gather her own thoughts into something resembling a coherent speech. "Mr Newman…" she said again.

"Darius," he corrected, and reached across the carriage to take her own gloved hand in his. "Call me Darius."

Bess looked down at their joined hands, at the way that they held steady even as the carriage bumped their bodies to and fro. "So you promised my mother that you would take care of me," she said slowly, and saw, out of the corner of her eye, Mr Newman nodding. "But are you sure that marriage was what was meant by such a promise?"

"My promise was given as a friend, it is true. But are the two really so different? We are friends now, Bess, are we not? And we would be greater friends still if you were to accept now. Instead of going back to that school—instead of continuing to hire yourself out—you could come to Hampshire with me. *You* could do a lot of good there, too. You would be my partner in everything. And your life, Bess: your life would not have to change in a material way.

What you have been used to all your life, with your mother and father; your life with me would not be so very different. You would have time to yourself, time to reflect and read and study. But, whenever you wish it, I could be by your side."

She had had her answer ready, but it was as though he had cast a spell over her. Suddenly she could see everything he was describing; she could see them living together and working side-by-side. She saw Mr Newman, shut up in his study writing a sermon, and herself knocking at the door with a cup of tea; as she came in, he would turn around in his chair and talk with her about what he was writing. It was a scene that she had observed between her parents many times during her childhood, but she did not know that it had burrowed itself so deeply inside her; she had not expected that, as it surfaced again now, it should make her feel happy and sad at the same time.

"Well, Bess?" said Mr Newman, who had been watching her intently all the while. "What do you say?"

Bess drew herself out of her own reverie, with all the discomfort and reluctance of one dragging oneself out of a warm bed on a winter's morning. Looking out the window, she saw that they had just passed a sign for Bradford. She turned her gaze to her and Mr Newman's joined hands.

"I would like to ask you a question now," she said. "And if you are indeed my friend, you will answer honestly."

"Of course." Mr Newman's voice was low.

"Do you still have Miss Foster's glove?"

"Her *glove?*"

"The one that she lost, months ago. The one that you took, one day." Bess met his gaze and saw that his face had blanched. "Yes, I saw that, too. Just as I saw you two, yesterday. Just as I have seen everything else that has passed between you, for all the time that you and I have known each other."

"Everything else?" Mr Newman burst out. "But there is nothing between us!"

"And what about what you just told me? What of the promises you made her?"

"It was all a dreadful mistake; I was carried away by my own sympathy. I felt for her, in her grief. I wanted to comfort her. She is so young still, so unfitted for life's challenges…"

"She is not so much younger than me," Bess pointed out.

"But there could not be a greater difference between you. Do you think she could come with me to Hampshire, and live as a minister's wife? It would not be possible."

"No," Bess agreed. "Because whoever she marries will inherit her father's estate."

"But it is not just that. If I were to allow myself to be carried away, once more—if I were to make the mistake of marrying her—I would soon regret it. She would regret it. She must marry someone in her own circle, someone who is accustomed to the same kind of life that she is."

"But perhaps she does not want that."

"She doesn't know what she wants," Mr Newman returned at once.

There was a roughness in his voice, at that moment, a certain quality that dissolved the spell that his words had cast on her, before. Bess was able to remove her hand from his and look at him quite calmly. The carriage was slowing now, as it approached the train station where she would continue on to Leeds.

"Do I understand you?" Mr Newman said, quietly. "Are you refusing me again?"

Bess nodded. He dragged his gaze away from her, but she kept her eyes fixed on his face as she spoke. "You will thank me for this, one day. Not today, but someday soon, when your feelings become as clear to yourself as they are to me."

"What makes you so sure?" he asked, and at this question, Bess was forced to think for a moment.

"Because I have felt what you feel now," she said at last. "Towards another. And it is not something to be ignored or waved away. It is not something you can run from."

NO HORIZON

When Bess had still been a child, forced by the indisposition of her mother to act as though she were the adult—since, after Mr Lanyard's death, there had been no one left in the world to advocate for them—the decisions that she had made, day by day, to ensure their survival, had never given her a moment's doubt. They had been necessary; they had not been something to agonise over later. Her first refusal of Mr Newman had been like that, too, at least in that it had not given her pain later on; she had had little doubt then, either, that she was acting right.

But the second time that she said no, and set out again alone into a barren world, she had no such comfort to ease her way.

Everything conspired to disappoint her; her reception at the school, after her bereavement, was not as kind as she had hoped. Her long absence from teaching had blunted her abilities, and she found herself stumbling through her lessons. Leeds had none of that charm that it had acquired shortly before her last departure from it; she realised that the charm had really all been Tom's.

Every night before she went to sleep, it was Mr Newman's face that came before her mind's eye, and his look of disappointment as she refused him. Bess would wonder then how she could have been right, and would toss and turn for at least an hour, going over their many conversations together, before she could get to sleep. In the morning, instead of feeling refreshed, she would look out of her window with weary eyes. She would see a white sky and grey buildings, and no horizon.

SUMMER

Spring slipped into summer without any material change in the weather, or so it seemed; even the trees in the city parks did not seem any greener than they had a month before. The school closed, and Bess packed up her things and headed back to Ashford Hall, where she had been invited to spend the holidays with Laura. She planned to stay there only a month, to her friend's disappointment; she could not justify spending the whole summer idle and had accepted a temporary position with a family in Bradford until the school in Leeds started up again.

Bess found her friend as dispirited as she was. Mr Newman had accepted the post in Hampshire, and his absence was most keenly felt in the neighbourhood. The new curate was disappointing; he never visited any of the poor families in the parish and could only be seen at the service on Sundays, after which he would seemingly vanish into thin air.

Bess missed Mr Newman's conversation, and his quiet, considering way of listening to what she had to say; she realised, now that she had lost it, how rare it was to find that in the company of any man. As for Laura, Bess was sure that the absence was felt by her, too, though her friend never once mentioned Mr Newman by name. Often the two young ladies would sit together in silence, each wrapped in her own thoughts of the past, each unable to voice what she felt—because to do so would give name to a feeling too lonely to be shared.

Over that summer, there were many admirers of the new heiress of Ashford Hall, some of them rich, a few of them handsome, one or two of them charming. It was some consolation to Bess to see the assurance with which Laura turned each of them away, and the way her friend never seemed to agonise over any of those refusals later; sometimes, even when the name of one such young gentleman was mentioned to her, she would not recall whom it referred to right away. Observing this, Bess felt a renewed confidence in her own refusal of Mr Newman, and though she was still far from what might be called happy, she at least slept better than she had during that grey month in Leeds.

"How does it go between your two friends?" opened one of Tom's letters to her, after she had been back at Ashford for nearly a month. It was the first such letter that she had received since she had left Leeds, though Bess herself was falling off in her own habits of correspondence.

She still thought of Tom every day, but she could feel his presence receding from her life; he shared none of her same concerns, knew none of the same people and had a very different future before him. "I won't speak any more plainly," the letter ran on, "as I know you have sworn me to secrecy in this matter. I will just say that I hope the clergyman and the heiress come to their senses. More unlikely unions have occurred, you know." Bess could not help but smile at this, and she sensed Laura look up from her sewing, curious at the expression on her friend's face.

"Will you come to Branledge, at last?" Tom's letter wound up by asking. "I have issued this invitation to you so many times that I feel like a parrot. And each time, you have very kindly—very firmly—very prudently, I am sure, refused. It would not be proper, you say, for you to accept my invitation, when we are both unmarried. Well, you might be right there—" Here Bess's heart skipped a beat, and she chided herself a moment later as she read the words that followed. "—but I have not run out of patience quite yet. And that is why you will shortly be receiving a letter from my sister, who simply *longs* to be acquainted with you, and who has decided to invite a stranger to her house, by some spontaneous impulse that has absolutely nothing to do with her brother's urging.

"You will like Branledge, I think. There are woods here, greener than the woods in your part of the country.

197

There's a lake, which is absolute heaven at this time of year: I can just see you sitting there on the bank, with a book in your hand. There's a rose garden, and a window seat in the morning room overlooking it; I can see you sitting there, too. So come along, Bess, and stop putting me off. Watch out for my sister's letter.

Yours, &c.,

Tom."

FOLLOW THE HEART

Miss Felicia Steele's letter did arrive, without delay. She wrote well, with none of her brother's careless, distracted style, as she invited Bess, very politely and correctly, to stay at Branledge, where they might become better acquainted. Bess promptly wrote a letter of refusal that was just as prompt and correct and was getting ready to bring it to the post office when Laura rushed into the drawing room.

Her friend was flushed and excited, the look in her eyes so bright and wild that Bess, alarmed, forgot her letter and came forward to take Laura's hands. "What's the matter, dear? What has happened?"

"He's here," Laura gasped. "Mr Newman's here. He's downstairs, Andrews has just shown him into the parlour. Oh, what am I to do, Bess, what am I to do? Why should he come all the way here, when he's supposed to be in Hampshire?"

"You must go and speak to him," Bess said after a moment.

"But what if it's not what I think? What if he's here on some business or other?"

"Then the sooner you go to talk to him, the sooner you will find out, and then the worst of it will be over."

"And what if it *is* what I think? What if he has come to ask me…"

Laura did not finish her sentence, but stared at Bess, as though waiting for some reply that would give her the certainty she needed. "… to ask you to marry him?" Bess finished.

"Yes, what if he asks me that? What on earth am I to say?"

"You must say whatever you feel is right."

"Oh come, now, Miss Lanyard, that's not proper advice!" Laura tugged at her hands with some of her old petulance. "Tell me what you *really* think."

Bess gazed at her friend. "I think," she said, "that I am not the person to give you advice. I could tell you to go downstairs now and face it, because you might have a chance of being happy if you do. I could tell you to do that, to tell you to do what I think to be right. But as I have not done it myself—*will* not do it myself… I don't see that I can lecture *you* on your own happiness, or the best way of achieving it."

"Bess," said Laura, and embraced her. "Bess," she said again against her shoulder. "I'll go down now, and face him, I swear. Just let me stay with you for a minute or two more. Let me stay here, where things make sense, where nothing has to change, where I don't have to feel this all over again —this thing I thought I was past."

Bess returned her friend's embrace, and said nothing, her mind suddenly far away.

Mr Newman proposed to Laura that day, and Bess did not post her letter of refusal to Miss Steele.

THE LONG ROAD

Branledge Hall was farther from home than she had ever travelled before. Tom might have been able to imagine her there, as he had said in his letter, but Bess herself could not. His world was one that she did not know, one into which she had never strayed before. She was not even sure if she would be allowed into it, once she arrived.

Miss Steele's letter of acknowledgement did arrive after Bess had sent her acceptance, and a date was arranged, and she decided which train she was going to take and wrote to the family in Bradford regretting that she was no longer available to take the temporary position.

But despite all of these very concrete arrangements, Bess could not shake the fear that this was all some joke with Tom, to invite a poor clergyman's daughter to stay with him and his sister at Branledge, so that they might laugh at her ways. She knew him; at least she was fairly sure she knew him, and she knew that he would not do such a thing. So why was the only picture that would come to her mind, when she tried to imagine herself at Branledge, that of her standing outside a set of locked gates, unable to get in?

Bess read and reread Tom's letters to her, as the day of her departure drew closer and closer, trying to see if she had mistaken something somewhere, as though she expected to find some single line of his that she had overlooked before; some sentiment that would make it absolutely, indisputably clear that he regarded her only as a friend, that his inviting her to Branledge was just some whim.

She didn't find anything, of course. Nothing became clearer, except that she was getting more and more afraid at the prospect of her long and lonely journey south.

It was useless to ask her friends for advice. They, being happy themselves, could only advise her to seek out her own happiness, too. Mr Newman, no longer labouring under the weight of a hidden ardour, smiled a great deal more than he had used to do.

Instead of wearing a pained expression whenever Laura entered the room, as he had done before, he made no attempt now to hide his affection, and as she spoke he would fix his eyes on her face, with a look of happy concentration. Her feelings were plainer still; for the first week or so after his proposal, she was almost as impossible as she had been back when she had first started to pursue him, and Bess could only be glad that she was no longer charged with her education—for it would have been impossible to get Laura to put her mind to anything during that time. But soon her feelings settled into some kind of calm, as she and her betrothed began to talk of their future, and how they were to manage to make a life together when their wants and needs were quite different.

Bess had no doubt that they could manage it; one only had to look in their faces to know. But perhaps she had always been a romantic, while pretending to be practical and prudent. Perhaps that was why she had turned down a perfectly good position and was about to embark on what might be a wild goose chase.

What waited for her if things at Branledge came to nothing? There were her friends in Ashford, but Bess might find their happiness hard to bear after her own disappointment. There was the school at Leeds in September, but Bess might find *that* hard to bear, too, with all the memories of Tom offered up at that place. That time with him was one that made her happy when she thought of it, now—but how was she going to think of it in a week's time, in a month's time? Would she want to remember it at all?

BRANLEDGE

Bess was so worn down by all this back and forth by the day of her departure, she just wanted it all to be over. She packed her things with a heavy heart, bid goodbye to her friends at the train station in Bradford, and climbed into her second-class carriage. She kept her valise between her feet as the carriage filled up, emptied, and filled up again around her. She fell asleep, instead of watching the changing landscape outside the window, and each train stop, as it was announced, drifted into her dreams. The names became more and more unfamiliar. Hearing at last, "Bath!" Bess jerked awake.

The train was slowing as it came into the station, and as they drew along the platform, Bess saw a familiar figure standing there.

She blinked and looked again. He was looking around, too, but did not see her yet.

He looked so handsome and distinguished that he drew admiring gazes from the other people on the platform, and from the other passengers as they began to disembark, and still Bess had not moved from her seat. She could not believe that he was really here for her—but there he was, still looking around, perhaps wondering if she had slipped past him somehow, in the crowd.

Bess wished that she could slip away now. She wished that she was back with her friends in Ashford. Her hands, as she slowly stood, were slippery with sweat and she could barely keep a grip on her valise. Her heart, as she walked down the carriage, was thumping so hard that she could hear a kind of whistle in her ears.

Then she heard another whistle: the train whistle, and she broke into a run, stepping out onto the platform just as the porter was about to close the door. "Sorry, miss," he said as she jumped down beside him, and she murmured her own apologies, already looking past him.

The crowd of passengers had begun to clear by now, and Tom at last saw her. He smiled. Bess, trembling, smiled back.

They were still too far away from one another to speak, but Bess could see, as Tom approached her at a quick stride, that he was getting ready to say something. She was getting ready, too. She was ready to be happy, or disappointed. By the look on Tom's face as he drew up to her, she was beginning to know which one it was going to be.

He took her valise from her slippery hands, passed it to his left hand, and offered her his right arm. Bess took it, and they walked down the platform together. All she wanted to look at was his face, but she forced herself to look around, to take in where they were. And as she did so, she thought she glimpsed for a moment, in the crowd, a man with her father's broad shoulders and long, lean frame: and, by his side, a woman with her mother's black hair and neat, dark blue coat.

In another moment, they had turned around and she could see by their faces that they were only strangers. But she smiled at them, and they watched her in incomprehension, until Tom's voice brought her attention back to him, where it would stay—Bess hoped—for a long time to come.

THE PROPOSAL BESS HAD BEEN WAITING FOR

The proposal came very soon after their exit from the station.

Tom had contrived an elaborate scheme in which a lavish meal at Branledge would be followed with a walk in the grounds during which the words he had been bursting to say would finally be spoken.

But the words could wait no longer.

With Branledge Hall still far away, the dirty pavement outside the station became the hallowed ground for Tom's proposal.

With impatient crowds of travellers bustling past them, Tom's own impatience could wait no longer.

Falling to one knee, and with tears in his eyes, he spoke the words Bess had so long yearned to hear.

"Dear Bess, will you do me the honour of becoming my wi…" was all he needed to utter.

Without hesitation, and with not a single doubt in her heart little Bess said, "Yes".

THANK YOU FOR CHOOSING A PUREREAD BOOK!

We hope you enjoyed the story, and as a way to thank you for choosing PureRead we'd like to send you this free book, and other fun reader rewards…

Click here for your free copy of Whitechapel Waif
PureRead.com/victorian

Thanks again for reading.
See you soon!

HAVE YOU READ?

THE COAL SCAVENGER'S DAUGHTER

Now that you have read 'Little Bess' why not lose yourself in another heartwarming Victorian Romance. Bess was not the only one to reach out a generous hand of kindness to a helpless soul and see her destiny change.

A young girl called Milcah also saw God's hand work in a powerful way when her father's kind heart saved the life of a stranger...

O n a chilly day, Milcah's father returns home with the body of an unconscious stranger in his cart. Milcah's father found the man drifting in the river and managed to save him.

Although the family barely have enough food to feed themselves, let alone to help another, Milcah's father tells his children that they must always help a person in need, regardless of who they are or how needy they themselves might be.

Milcah takes the lesson to heart, and after a few days under her care, the stranger wakes.

He barely speaks and **then he vanishes in the night**. The family assumes that they will never see him again.

Little do they suspect that their kindness to this one stranger will eventually change their lives forever.

Here for your enjoyment is the beginning of Little Milcah's story...

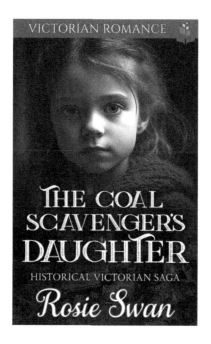

Sheffield, England, 1865

Milcah Fox, age nine and a half, was the oldest of seven children, with an eighth sibling on the way. Her father was a peasant farmer, and although her family owned its own little scrap of land in their village near Sheffield in the North of England, the half-acre had stubborn soil, and it barely produced enough to feed the family, let alone to sell. Her father made his money labouring on other people's land, while her mother did what laundry and mending she could find in their village, where the mine owners and businessmen were far outnumbered by poor miners and farmers.

The family could not afford to send any of the children to school, and so Milcah could neither read nor write, but she did not feel the lack of it. She would not have had time for schooling, anyway, when her daylight hours were split between taking care of her younger siblings while her mother worked or rested, and scavenging around the coal mines, searching for any dropped pieces of coal that the family might be able to sell.

It was a poverty-filled existence, but Milcah had never known anything different, and family life was so full of love and laughter that she was perfectly content with the little world that life had given her. Her mother worked hard to make their food stretch as far as it could, creating the most delicious meals from the humblest of ingredients. Her father toiled all day, but he always made it home before the children went to bed, so that he could hear all their jokes and news from the day and tell them another installment of his epic bedtime story of daring knights and terrifying dragons.

If Milcah's mother and father were worried about how they would feed the newest baby on the way, they did not mention it where Milcah could hear. Neither did they mention their concern over Milcah's mother's strange tiredness and breathlessness, which was far worse than it had been for any of her previous pregnancies.

But, Milcah's father reasoned to her mother, after all the little ones had gone to sleep, that they were both older now, and caring for children while carrying another was tiring work. It was only natural that Milcah's mother would find pregnancy a little harder at thirty than she had at twenty, and there was little to worry about when she was so experienced in the battle of childbirth now. First she had had Milcah, and then three sets of twins—Rachel and Leah, Scott and Russell, and Dale and Grace—and all of them had been healthy with a fierce pair of lungs to herald their arrival in the world. Based on the size of Milcah's mother's bump, they would only be blessed with one child this time, and one baby would be easy after caring for so many pairs, especially now that Milcah was old enough to be of help.

"But *when* will the baby come?" Milcah asked her mother for the fifth evening in a row, when her mother had been pregnant seemingly forever.

"Soon, Milcah," her mother said with a smile, as she had the past several times. "Any day now."

"Tomorrow?" Milcah asked.

Her mother laughed. "I don't know, Milcah," she said. "The baby will arrive when he or she decides to arrive. They can't be rushed, and they don't follow anyone's schedule except their own."

"But it *might* be tomorrow?"

Her mother ruffled her hair. "Yes, Milcah," she said. "It might be tomorrow. It might be a week. It might be a while yet. You never quite know."

"I hope it's soon," Milcah said.

"So do I, little one," her mother replied. "I'm getting too large to walk."

Her father chuckled. "You'll have to take good care of your mama once the baby comes, Milcah. She'll be exhausted. She'll need you more than ever."

Milcah nodded seriously and curled up against her mother's side, resting her head atop her huge stomach. Her mother wrapped an arm around her, pulling her even closer.

"What about me?" her younger sister Rachel asked, scrambling across the room to join them.

"You as well," their father said. He picked up his seven-year-old daughter and swung her onto his lap. "The whole family will need all of you."

Rachel's twin sister Leah ran after her and clambered onto their father's lap too. The four younger siblings were all asleep in their corner of the room, but the three oldest were all allowed to stay up a little later, and no matter how tired Milcah might be, she could not bear to miss a single moment with her parents and sisters, not even to sleep.

"I hope it's a girl!" Leah said. "Girls are much more fun than boys."

"Whether they're a boy or a girl, I know you'll welcome them and love them just the same," their father said.

Leah nodded. "But a sister would be better please."

Their mother laughed. "All right, Leah," she said. "I'll see what I can do. But for now, I think it's bedtime for all of you. Your father and I as well, I think. It's been a long day."

"Tell us another story before we go to sleep!" Rachel said, wrapping her arms around her father's neck. "Please."

He chuckled. "I don't think your brothers and sister would like it if they found out I'd told you the next part of the story while they were sleeping, do you?"

"It doesn't have to be about Sir Boldheart," Milcah said quickly. "It could be another story."

Rachel gave her an annoyed look that suggested that 'another story' was not what she had had in mind, but her expression brightened again when her father went, "All right, all right. If it'll get you all to sleep with good dreams. Have I ever told you the story of Sir Boldheart's childhood friend, Lord Elroy?"

All three girls shook their heads.

"Well," their father began, "he was a cowardly boy, but one day, he wandered into the forest too deep…."

Milcah drifted to sleep in her mother's arms, listening to her father's soothing voice.

The next morning, Milcah's mother looked a little pale, but she smiled and hugged her daughter as Milcah scurried off to the mines. Never had she wanted to stay home with her mama more, but Milcah knew that if she did not go, there would be less food at the end of the day, and her mama and papa would almost certainly choose to go hungry themselves to give what food there was to the children.

Besides, Milcah knew that when the baby came, she and her sisters would be sent out of the house to stay with one of their neighbours. Last time, it had been old Mrs, Smith, a kindly widow whose grandchildren had all long since grown, and so who never missed an opportunity to fuss over the children or listen to their stories. Milcah thought she wouldn't mind sitting around Mrs. Smith's hearth with all her siblings, staying up far later into the night than they were ever usually allowed, waiting to find out whether the new baby was a boy or a girl and hearing stories of when Mrs. Smith. was young, when England was ruled by a prince, not a queen, and there were no steam engines to fuel with coal, so the mines did not even exist.

Milcah walked in the direction of the mines, her mind full of thoughts of new babies and of the strangeness of a world that existed long before she herself had been born. But the mine soon jolted her out of her daydreams. It was a terribly noisy place, with the thunder, or lift, that brought men up and down from far below the surface, and the rattle of the wheels of carts of coal. Pit ponies, half-blind from their existence in the darkness of the tunnels, neighed and snorted, and men shouted greetings and instructions to one another over the chaos.

Milcah had never been down into the mines themselves, but she still felt a little chill of fear every time she saw men step into the great iron lift and begin to descend. She could not fully imagine the horror of being trapped underground, with tons and tons of rock and earth separating you from the open sky, forced to dig deeper and hope that the walls would hold. The men would emerge from the mines with their faces blackened, blinking at the rush of sunlight, and Milcah always shivered to imagine how hard it must have been for them to breathe down there in the dark.

Milcah sometimes overheard her mama say that if anything went wrong while a man was down in the mines, only God could save him. "It doesn't matter a man's wits, or his skill, or how careful he might be. He can do little to save himself when the air is gone and the ceiling is falling in. And while we trust in the Lord," she said, with a sad shake of her head, "the masters should use the brains and pity He gave them to care for their men, instead of leaving them to hope for miracles."

Milcah did not think she was meant to hear these speeches. She was certain her mama would have spoken more quietly if she had known her daughter was awake. Occasionally, the topic of conversation arose when *something* happened in the mines—some event that the adults would not tell the children much about, but which shook the ground something fierce and meant that some workers would never return home again. More often, Milcah overheard this speech when her father tentatively raised the idea that *he* might find employment in the mines to better feed the family. After her mother's panicked lecture, he would not raise the idea for quite a while again.

But the area around the mines was safe enough, or so Milcah always thought. If it wasn't, her mama would never have allowed her to go there. You had to keep your wits about you, because there was so much *activity*, and the men had little time to worry about whether a little girl might be in their path as they transported their black treasure out of the mines.

By the end of the day, Milcah's skin would always be smeared with black, and her body would ache from all the walking back and forth and crouching to collect little fragments of coal from the ground. She could always feel the coal dust in the air, too, scraping her throat and making her cough, but she never complained, knowing she was lucky to be up here under the open sky and not down in the pits and tunnels below.

Some children were far less lucky. Young boys and girls were used to squeeze into spaces too small for any grown man, and Milcah knew of children who worked as door keepers, spending their days sitting in the dark on the edge of the tracks, waiting for the signal to open the doors to allow the carts to pass. Sometimes children fell asleep while alone in the dark, and then when the cart finally came….

Yes, Milcah thought. She was incredibly lucky.

It was midway through the afternoon when Milcah spotted her sister Leah racing across the mines toward her. Leah never came to the mines; she was too scared of the noise and the chaos, and instead always stayed home with mama to help with the mending and keep an eye on the younger ones. But Leah was running through the yard now, her braided hair flying out behind her, paying no mind to the racket and bustle around her.

"Milcah!" she shouted, loudly enough that several people looked up.

Milcah hurried towards her. "I'm here, Leah," she said. "What's wrong?"

Leah skidded to a stop in front of her, gasping for breath. "Something's wrong with mama," she said. "I can't find papa, and there's something wrong with mama."

Terror flooded Milcah. She did not pause to ask any more questions. She set off running in the direction of home, Leah scrambling to keep pace beside her.

"Is it the baby?" Milcah gasped, as they skidded out of the mines.

"I don't know!" Leah cried. "She was screaming, and I didn't know what to do, and she sent me out of the house—"

Rachel was sitting a little way beyond the front of their home with the younger twins in the dirt around her. She was hugging little three-year-old Grace, while Scott and Russell traced patterns in the earth.

"Mrs. Smith is here," Rachel said in a hushed voice as her sisters approached. "She said we should stay out here...."

"Mama's been crying," Grace mumbled, her face pressed against Rachel's shoulder.

"But she hasn't in a little while now," Rachel said, patting her youngest sister on the head. "Maybe she's feeling better."

"Did papa come home?" Milcah asked. Her sisters shook their heads.

Dread weighed down Milcah's stomach. "I'll go in," she said. "I'll see if she's all right."

But as Milcah walked up the front path, the door opened, and Mrs. Smith stepped out. Her hands and dress were stained with blood, and her pale face was stained with tears. She stared at the sky for a moment, not seeming to notice Milcah's presence at all, and wiped under her eyes with the back of her hand. She left blood smeared on her cheek.

"Mrs. Smith?" Milcah said.

Mrs. Smith jumped. Her wide eyes fell on Milcah. "Milcah," she said.

"What's wrong?" Milcah asked, but she felt almost certain that she did not want to know the answer. "Where's mama?"

Mrs. Smith looked at her with such pity that Milcah immediately wanted to take the question back, to never have asked it, to never have even *thought* it. But the words were out in the world now, and even before Mrs Smith spoke, Milcah knew what her answer would be.

"I'm so sorry, dear," Mrs Smith said. "But she's with the Lord now. She's at peace."

Milcah began to sob.

What will happen to Milcah and her siblings? Does God have a plan to restore this family? Can their faith carry them through?

Discover all in the #1 Bestselling book, The Coal Scavenger's Daughter.

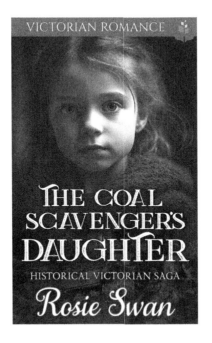

Start Reading Now

LOVE VICTORIAN ROMANCE?

If you enjoyed this story why not continue straight away with other books in our PureRead Victorian Romance library?

Read them all...

Victorian Slum Girl's Dream

Poor Girl's Hope

The Lost Orphan of Cheapside

Born a Workhouse Baby

The Lowly Maid's Triumph

Poor Girl's Hope

The Victorian Millhouse Sisters

Dora's Workhouse Child

Saltwick River Orphan

Workhouse Girl and The Veiled Lady

OUR GIFT TO YOU

AS A WAY TO SAY THANK YOU WE WOULD LOVE TO SEND YOU THIS BEAUTIFUL STORY FREE OF CHARGE.

Click here for your free copy of Whitechapel Waif

PureRead.com/victorian

At PureRead we publish books you can trust. Great tales without smut or swearing, but with all of the mystery and romance you expect from a great story.

Be the first to know when we release new books, take part in our fun competitions, and get surprise free books in your inbox by signing up to our free VIP Reader list.

As a welcome gift you'll receive the story of the Whitechapel Waif straight to your inbox...

Click here for your free copy of Whitechapel Waif

PureRead.com/victorian

Printed in Great Britain
by Amazon